NEW YORK REVIEW BOOKS
C L A S S I C S

T0022444

OUR PHILOSOPHER

GERT HOFMANN (1931–1993) was born in Limbach,
Saxony. For two decades, he taught German literature at
universities across Europe, Britain, and the United States,
composing radio plays in his spare time. In 1979, he turned
his hand to fiction. In the years that remained to him, he
wrote thirteen novels and short-story collections, including
The Parable of the Blind, *The Film Explainer*, and *Lichtenberg and the Little Flower Girl*. He was awarded the
Ingeborg Bachmann Prize and the Alfred Döblin Prize.

ERIC MACE-TESSLER has lived in Germany and Switzerland for three decades. He taught literature until his recent
retirement.

MICHAEL HOFMANN, the son of Gert Hofmann, is a
German-born, British-educated poet, critic, and translator.
His most recent books are *One Lark*, *One Horse* (poems)
and *Messing About in Boats* (essays). For New York Review
Books he has translated several works, including Alfred
Döblin's *Berlin Alexanderplatz*, and edited an anthology of
writing by Malcolm Lowry, *The Voyage That Never Ends*.

OUR PHILOSOPHER

GERT HOFMANN

Translated from the German by
ERIC MACE-TESSLER

Introduction by
MICHAEL HOFMANN

NEW YORK REVIEW BOOKS

New York

THIS IS A NEW YORK REVIEW BOOK
PUBLISHED BY THE NEW YORK REVIEW OF BOOKS
207 East 32nd Street, New York, NY 10016
www.nyrb.com

Originally published in the German language as *Veilchenfeld*.

This translation was originally published in the United Kingdom by
CB Editions in 2020. It appears here in a slightly revised form.

First published as a New York Review Books Classic in 2023.

Library of Congress Cataloging-in-Publication Data
Names: Hofmann, Gert, author. | Mace-Tessler, Eric, translator. | Hofmann,
  Michael, 1957 August 25, writer of introduction.
Title: Our philosopher / by Gert Hofmann; translated by Eric Mace-Tessler;
  introduction by Michael Hofmann.
Other titles: Veilchenfeld. English
Description: New York: New York Review Books, [2023] | Series: New York
  Review Books classics |
Identifiers: LCCN 2023004647 (print) | LCCN 2023004648 (ebook) |
  ISBN 9781681377582 (paperback) | ISBN 9781681377599 (ebook)
Subjects: LCGFT: Novels.
Classification: LCC PT2668.O376 V4513 2023 (print) | LCC PT2668.O376
  (ebook) | DDC 833/.914—dc23/eng/20230206
LC record available at https://lccn.loc.gov/2023004647
LC ebook record available at https://lccn.loc.gov/2023004648

ISBN 978-1-68137-758-2
Available as an electronic book; ISBN 978-1-68137-759-9

Printed in the United States of America on acid-free paper.
10 9 8 7 6 5 4 3 2 1

INTRODUCTION

WHEN I think of the lugubrious, pessimistic, and altogether funny-fantastical oeuvre of my father, Gert Hofmann, I think of Kleist's observation that an arch remains standing because its stones all want to fall at the same time. Hofmann was an acclaimed master of that spectral form, the radio play. Most of his life, he worked as a German *Lektor* at universities in England, Scotland, the United States, and Slovenia. With a certain amount of pride, he raised a family. He came to fiction late, when they were mostly gone. His first novel, *Die Fistelstimme* (The Falsetto), was published in 1980, when he was almost fifty. He was conscious of having to make up for lost time. His contemporaries were famous and successful (some; others, of course, were obscure in their own kitchens). He had little in common with younger writers. And so, in the 1980s and 1990s he wrote and published a dozen or so books of fiction at the rate of one a year. The completed manuscript of *Die kleine Stechardin* (translated into English as *Lichtenberg and the Little Flower Girl*) was on his desk when he died on July 1, 1993, thirty years ago and far too young. In his eulogy, Michael Krüger, the last of his several German publishers, spoke of "this friendly, driven man." Actes Sud, his French publisher, lamented "the premature disappearance of a visionary and cosmopolitan writer."

Within that Kleistian arch, *Our Philosopher* (*Notre Phi-losophe* in French, a title he greatly liked; *Veilchenfeld* in the original, and in Ian McEwan's stunning reference to the book in his own novel *Lessons*, and then in a later article) occupies something like the capstone. In terms both of the years of his accelerated and abbreviated career, and of its place among his books, it comes squarely in the middle: published in 1986, and the sixth or seventh of his major publications. Halfway. *Nel mezzo.*

Further, for reasons both accidental and deliberate, my father's writing evolved (in my sense of them) from "grammar-books" to "word- or phrasebooks." The early novels and stories got him a rather undesirable reputation as a difficult writer, a virtuoso, one for the few. He operated with layerings of reported speech and reported writing, so that a sentence might end—if it ever chose to, and remember, German, so verbs at the end—with "he said, he thought, he wrote." There is still some of that Russian doll protocoling in *Our Philosopher*, but it is already making way as a technique for an altogether more casual, informal, unexplained collage of speech, in which the figures are made up of words, rather as the figures in Philip Guston paintings are made up of bandages. In fact, the spoken words have more reality than the speakers. Think radio plays with children's angelic voices. Eccentric interrogations. Think innocents without innocence, truth from the lips of babes and sucklings. The piercing treble. Think *Weltmaschine* (the title of a story he published in the same year as *Our Philosopher*), which grinds passing small. Think of Veilchenfeld, with his bandaged head, and holes left for the eyes, the mouth. The nose—good question.

Our Philosopher has a further kind of centrality in that my father wrote his books on one of two subjects: artists and childhood, the childhood very often based on his own, raised by his mother and grandfather in the small town of Limbach-Oberfrohna in provincial Saxony, as may be read in *Our Conquest* or *The Film Explainer*. *Our Philosopher* combines elements of both. There is the artist, which Veilchenfeld certainly is, with philosophy seeping into ancillaries of painting and music: the bookshelves, the string quartet, the piano, the sketchbooks. Even that provocatively unidentifiable notion, "our philosopher," suffers further diffusion. "Our philosopher"—how can anyone possibly tell: a pipe, a way of scratching his chin or staring into space? As though it had been "our baker" or "our newsagent" or even "our neighbor." The phrase is in fact an oxymoron: Precise and then uncertain. Possessive and then elusive. A hand clutching at a cloud. Or punching it. One way of reading the book is to see it as the "we" expelling the philosopher from their midst. His identification and then expulsion. Call it intellectual cleansing. His extrusion.

And then there are the children. Hans, our boy narrator, precocious and still in single figures, and his even younger sister, Gretel. Of course. We are in a German fairy tale of sorts. The children are the book's true philosophers, always questing for the last word, never without a question or an objection on their lips.

And me? my sister asks.
You can't either.

Our Philosopher straddles—or yokes—the two subjects. It is part family drama (as *Luck* would be, later), part *Künstlerroman*. Or part "chronicle of a death foretold" (my father admired the novella by Gabriel García Márquez; it may even have served him as a model here), and part *Entwicklungsro-man*. This last of course in the bleakest and most ironical way possible. I'm not being fanciful or sentimental when I think perhaps Hans, having effectively killed him (spoiler alert—not much), will one day become Veilchenfeld. Out of guilt, but also—different sense—from conviction. He will come to understand that a life without annotated books, a piano, a sketchbook, is not really worth living. Maybe.

There is some limited interaction. Veilchenfeld spends an evening with Hans's family; Hans's father, the peg-leg veteran doctor, with his phantom pains, periodically sees to Veilchenfeld's heart ("which is no longer beating correctly"), and his head; Hans goes to him for drawing lessons; he sees and acknowledges him in public from time to time; he accedes, probably not understanding what he is doing, to his last request; he hangs around dangerously as Veilchenfeld's body is picked up by the undertakers—the scene with which the book begins and ends. In some ways, this isn't much; the two cogs are only intermittently touching. They are more like parts of separate stories. As I say, my father's two subjects. In other ways, though, it feels like a lot, and not really necessary at that, given that their one constant connection is Hans's lifelong curiosity about Veilchenfeld, which we take as a given, to the extent that his father early on warns him about it: "I really would prefer that you didn't think about him so much, says Father." The whole book thinks periodically about all sorts of other things (it is a distractable sort of book)—perhaps it even tries *not* to think about Veilchenfeld too much—but it does keep returning to him.

It does so in a macabre suburban setting. A secretly barbarous setting. Some conflation here of banality and monstrosity. An infernal machine and an "our town" that is so

characterful as to be anonymous. Or so bursting with ano-
nymity as to be characterful. One that prides itself on being,
of all things, heart-shaped. A foldaway set of houses, tene-
ments, streets and parks, official buildings, and happy happy
shrubs: the lilac in which Veilchenfeld is given to lurking,
the widowed beanpoles he perambulates around, already
under unspoken house arrest or "protective custody," an
elderberry, an apple tree. (Perhaps one remembers Brecht's
lines about a conversation about trees being tantamount to
a crime because it includes silence on so many other atroci-
ties?) Further afield, a brick factory, a quarry, a lake, just the
place for Sunday strolls. The central figure, with his consum-
mate harmlessness and his almost comically useless occupation, and the contrast between him and the healthy—although,
in point of fact, diseased and disfigured—world around him,
which is nothing if not useful in its productions: bricks and
stones, whips and jam, an extensive administrative machin-
ery and numerous finely calibrated, though in the end perfectly interchangeable, hostelries. It all feels as miniaturized,
as clarified, as a fairground, a puppet show, a board game.
The Austrian critic and Germanist Walter Grünzweig has
written of the *Realitätsverlust*—the loss both of realism and
of reality—that, he argues, constitutes the most character-
istic quality of my father's writing.

Here are some words that do not appear in *Our Philosopher*: Jew, Nazi, Brownshirt, Blackshirt, Hitler, Nuremberg,
Kristallnacht, victim, pogrom; nor, for that matter, minor-
ity, immigrant, race, persecution, lynching, Lives Matter,
ethnic cleansing (I could go on). The reason they are not
there is not because they have been suppressed but because
they are presumed. They are all over—or all under—the
book. In the invisible underpinnings of its events and scenes,

its queasy mix of poverty, sickness, banality, jollity, hatred, and violence. Why say what the reader knows already? Why not just supply the soundtrack—or speech ribbons—for the invisible and superior film in the reader's head? Where everything plays anyway: *Schauplatz Menschenkopf*, as my father said. Scene of the action, the human head.

I have forgotten how unconventional, how radical, how strange my father's books can be. They are like novels turned inside out, or on their heads, the inverse of novels. No plot, no character, no description, no action. No style. The point is not character revealing itself in action. The doctor and his wife, the father and mother, are they "good," are they sympathetic? His professional attention (of little objective value), her Veilchenfeld-induced colics. Redemptive? Or hypocritical? Even Hans, so compelled by Veilchenfeld, the one truly noteworthy presence in so much child-ordinariness; is his interest entirely benevolent? I think so, but would find it hard to prove in my father's almost post-psychological telling. It is strange to see any references to the "real" world. Only very occasionally. "The Condor Legion pilots." "The 18th of September, a Monday, around ten." (Which would put us, impossibly, in 1939, and after the invasion of Poland. But it only goes to show my father never cared about these things and will not have looked it up.) A smattering of places in and around Limbach. Helenenstrasse. Am hohen Hain. Bits of *realia*, not too much.

Senseless German reviewers complained that there was no proper philosophy, nothing plausible and detailed attached to Veilchenfeld, not understanding that it's not that sort of book, not understanding that it's not a documentary novel, that, as I remarked earlier, the real philosophers in it are Hans and Gretel with their incessant questions. (Isn't that what philosophers do? Ask questions?) The action seems to take place in a puppet theater, and to involve principally the misunderstandings and evasions and attempted obfuscations of speech. What a poor device the question is, and yet we have nothing better. It's the dialogue here that is load-bearing, the back and forth of the scenes, the macabrely echoing exchanges. Once I have people talking to each other, I'm away, my father would say. Besides, what's wrong with this as philosophy, a jazzy comic nihilism: "Instead, Herr Veilchenfeld cites or makes up the sentence about how life comes from the abyss and drags on for a while, and then retreats back into the abyss without trace or consequence."

A note on Eric Mace-Tessler's translation. He wrote to me many years ago, out of the blue, to discover whether I had an interest in translating *Our Philosopher* myself. I did not. I was happy to have translated my father's last three books. Other books had been translated by others before me—by Edna McCown, by the late Christopher Middleton. But Mr. Mace-Tessler had always wanted to work on *Veilchenfeld*, and he completed his translation, as we say in the profession, or better, in the calling, on spec. He did it for the noblest of reasons: that it might exist in English. He mulled over his translation for years, and reading it now, I can say that it is as careful and devoted a version as may be done. It was first published in London in 2020 by Charles Boyle in his CB Editions, which is how Ian McEwan came upon it, and now here it is in your hands, the reader's or purchaser's, or perhaps just the person's thinking about it.

—Michael Hofmann
March 2023

OUR PHILOSOPHER

Our philosopher has died suddenly. Our hearse collected him. The hearse drivers—no one knows who had them come—drove up to his place Monday morning on rubber wheels, silently, and they sprang from their box. We saw it ourselves.

We're leaning against Höhler's garden fence and aren't making ourselves dirty. The hearse drivers pull the coffin meant for Herr Veilchenfeld out of their large-wheeled, solemn and rickety hearse with a remarkable scraping noise that carries the length of Heidenstrasse, and disappear, after having tapped in passing on the feather-tufted neck of their little horse. Surely they don't want to go and get Herr Veilchenfeld? Yes, they are getting Herr Veilchenfeld! Only yesterday, around eight in the evening in middling weather, I saw him in his back garden, pale but standing amidst the lilac bushes. He was behind, not in front of, his garden wall, but we could see through the cracks. For, although it was known in our town that after his release Herr Veilchenfeld had moved out to us, and now lived in Heidenstrasse *without connections* (Mother), in the house with the bay window, he was more and more seldom to be seen in the last days.

Does he really still live here? we ask Father.

Yes, says Father, he is upstairs.

And what does he do?

He sits at his table.
And why doesn't he come down?

Because I feel more secure amongst my books than amongst my fellow countrymen, Herr Veilchenfeld always said to Mother across the narrow bit of garden, which he retraced with short steps time and again, and, under the brim of his black hat, he smiled at her out on the street.

If he had at least moved into a house with a larger garden, Mother said to Father. At the edge of town there are some. One's even empty up in Birkengasse. There he could have had his exercise without anyone seeing him. While here, where he lives now... It's always just the same six or seven paces he can walk here. He'll really go crazy, constantly walking around in circles.

And how was he supposed to know that one day he would not dare leave his garden when he wanted to have some exercise? Father asked her. Though he knew our philosopher well from his visits, Father also hadn't known at that time about leaving the garden.

Yes, said Mother, for a philosopher, he has changed a lot. Unfortunately, he's completely run down now, outwardly, and his nerves as well.

For it was not only when he did go into town sometimes, to buy bread perhaps, that Herr Veilchenfeld pulled his hat far down over his face and turned up his coat collar, so that at least he couldn't be recognised from a distance. He didn't even willingly go to our shops. And if he did go into a shop and the shop wasn't empty, he placed himself in a corner and let everyone go before him, even us. And he preferred to be looked after by Frau Bichler, even if she did *ruin him financially* (Mother) and often let him down. But if we did see him some time walking down the street, along the kerb as if it were a tightrope, he greeted us of course, but as if under torture, and he said every time: Please, don't tell anyone that you've seen me. The less said about me, the better. Or: I am only an apparition. Poof, I will vanish immediately! Or simply: Forget about me.

As things stand, it would be better if you didn't speak to him on the street any more, Mother always said, once we had passed him.

And say hello? we asked Mother. Should we still say hello to him?

No, said Mother, don't say hello either. Instead we should act as if we don't know him, as if he were already no longer present.

And if he says hello?

My God! Mother cried and flung up her arms, I'm sure that he won't be so tactless.

So that, when we saw him from far away—that was just after the *Deutscher Peter*—we no longer said hello to Herr Veilchenfeld, but instead looked down at the ground. But then when we reached him, we winked at him, so that he realised that we knew who he was. And Herr Veilchenfeld, as a sign that he forgave us, winked back. Sometimes he smiled too when he winked, though naturally only a little, and we went on, each to his own place.

Ever since two blocks of flats, in the shadows of which we now live, were built across from us in a single autumn, our house is smaller than it used to be. If someone who doesn't know it is looking for it, he can hardly find it. New patients who want to see Father first ask at the blocks of flats whether or not Father lives there. No, they are told, he lives over there in the little house. Oh, they say, really? They often don't ask at all and just go away. What these new buildings amount to in losses, no one would believe, Father says to Mother and to us, but he doesn't want to move, as he lacks the energy to do so. We also lack our sandbox now. When we heard that they wanted to take it from us, we howled with rage, though that didn't help at all. The fence was simply removed and a street was built through our garden and our sandbox, so that the tenants of the new buildings could get to their flats. Now you see only the street; the sandbox has disappeared. Also lacking: 1 maple, 1 walnut, 1 rabbit hutch for our annual rabbit named Puschel, which, because there's no longer a run, Father has not replaced. Also, now that we lack a horizon, we can no longer see the approach of a storm and we don't know what kind of weather there'll be the next day, or whether there'll be any at all, Father tells us. Instead we're showered by the furnace soot of thirty-eight families, so that our poor mother has to have everything washed twice, as she says. Many brick workers, all from the big city, now live above us, and for them everything here is too close. Father tells us there will also be many misunderstandings between us and them, as for example because of what one said to the other or didn't say.

On the day that the hearse comes for Herr Veilchenfeld, Mother pulls down the blinds in the evening but doesn't switch on the light. Instead we sit in the dark for a long time, and think again and again that we hear footsteps in front of the house. But we are mistaken, no doubt. Also, when it's time for it, Mother forgets about supper altogether. Mother, my little sister calls, why, you've forgotten about supper! But Mother doesn't answer her. She has sat down on the kitchen chair, but she isn't knitting either. Instead she lets her arms hang down on the right and left sides of the chair, where with the coming of dusk they are more and more invisible. Perhaps she has dozed off, or something much worse.

Mama, my sister calls, the light, the light! Mama, she calls, where are you?

Oh, says Mother, where should I be? I'm here, of course. And, as if she's on a school bench, she raises her hand to show my sister. And she means to get up too and go through the kitchen and finally turn the light on, but she keeps forgetting. Only when we can no longer make out her arms and her hands and her face in the darkness and Father comes back from his house calls and makes a great deal of noise in the hall with his artificial leg does Mother get up and switch on the light. Then the table is set too, but no one wants to eat anything.

Here, Mother says, and points to the food she's placed on the table and pushes it towards all of us, but Father shakes his head and says: Not now, perhaps later. And he lets a really long time pass by and then takes a slice of bread and cuts it into two equal pieces, but then instead of spreading something on them, he lifts the knife in the air and exclaims, Listen to me, there's more coming.

And what more's coming? my sister asks, and looks at the door.

What must come, will come, Father says, since he doesn't want to tell us what.

Then Mother lays the bread, which she took after Father did, back in the basket—she doesn't even cut it—and says something, but something completely different. She says that in other times a philosopher of Herr Veilchenfeld's status would have had a splendid funeral. Indeed he would have been entitled either to the simultaneous or subsequent sacrificial death of his connections and other members of his household, who naturally would not have wanted to survive him.

And why not? we ask.

Absolutely, she says.

But he didn't have any connections.

That makes no difference, she says.

Is that what you wanted to say just now? we ask Father.

In any case, Father says, I have no appetite and I'm going to lie down now. I had such a hard day, you wouldn't believe it. And he gets up and goes into his consulting room and he's eaten nothing today and indeed won't eat anything.

But you've eaten nothing at all, Mother calls after Father, everything is still there.

Quite so, says Father and shuts the door behind him and lies down. Once Father has lain down, it is immediately much quieter, although Father said nothing and didn't shout.

Will Frau Abfalter die too now, since Herr Veilchenfeld is dead? my sister asks Mother.

No, says Mother, not her. And she puts the bread, the sausage, and the cheese back in the kitchen cupboard. Now we keep going back and forth beside her between the table and the cupboard, asking what Father *really* meant when he said there's more coming, but Mother doesn't tell us. Perhaps she doesn't know herself. Perhaps she simply doesn't want to tell us. And then when we're put to bed and covered and

I ask her whether she won't at least tell us what she meant by *subsequent death*, she shakes her head. Oh, just that, somehow, she says.

On the afternoon of the festival, probably when Mother is already looking for us at the other end of town, Herr Veilchenfeld, with the black now somewhat decayed hat on his head, with his scarf wound around his neck—that is, as if prepared for a long trip which would take him far from our town—is in his garden, because here no one will see him when the parade with the music passes through Heidenstrasse. He also has his emergency bag with him, which he won't part with any more. He also has his doctoral diploma (*"summa cum laude"*) in his jacket pocket, right over his heart. In addition: the substitute for a passport, fifty marks in small bills, his birth certificate, his confirmation document, his police clearance, on which it is indicated that previous convictions are inapplicable, a photograph of his wife when young in a high-necked white blouse, and ten sugar cubes for quick energy, Mother says. In case he is suddenly relocated, she says, when we ask about it. And now quickly into the tub, the water will get cold, she calls, and she lets the water run.

And when will he be relocated? I ask and undress as slowly as possible.

Soon now, Mother says.

And why will he be relocated?

Because of what he thinks.

And what does he think? asks my little sister, who doesn't trust Herr Veilchenfeld.

But that, too, Mother can't tell her. She can't read his mind. He just thinks differently, she says.

And we, asks my sister, how do we think?

Like everyone.

Then we won't be relocated too?

No, says Mother. And now into the tub.

And what's in his emergency bag? I ask, when we're lying together in the tub, so that we can be done all in one go.

Oh, how should I know that? I haven't looked in it either, Mother says. Shirts and trousers and socks probably, just what one needs. And a couple of books, in order to pass the time. He's used to it now.

Later Mother has an attack because, as if she had guessed, it is in fact not Frau Abfalter, who never would have thought of such a thing, but Dr Magirius, Herr Veilchenfeld's former colleague and student, whose death follows his quite suddenly. To be sure, Dr Magirius was *weak on his legs* for a long time (Mother), but nevertheless was still *sufficiently eating and excreting* (Father). By lying down on the tracks of our provincial train on which he always came to us here, as Father said to Mother, when he came back from the investigation. And he is found—*with his thighs torn away*, having bled to death—by a railroad worker who was just checking the tracks. The engineer hadn't noticed anything at all. Then naturally they called Father at once; we unfortunately slept through it. Father got into his automobile and drove to the place they described to him. He had a look at everything, and from his doctor's bag took the forms that he always had ready, and filled them out while standing, and confirmed Herr Magirius' death, noting nothing about him, although of course he had known Herr Magirius. Indeed it's always like that with Father. Only seldom is anything noted: his voice, whether he's sad or happy, is invariably even-tempered.

When he returns, he stands at the house door for a long time with his doctor's bag, as if, after confirming the death of Herr Magirius, he didn't want to come back to us at all, but instead now wanted to go away as well, though he seemed still undecided as to where. It's only when he comes in after all and is sitting before us at the table and we ask him: Why Herr Magirius now too, Papa? that he loses his self-control and shouts at us that we shouldn't ask so much.

And think, I ask. May I think about him?

Now that I can't forbid, but I really would prefer that you didn't think about him so much, says Father.

But if a person doesn't think about somebody any more, surely he forgets him, I say.

In any case, I would prefer that you didn't think about him so much, Father exclaims and hurries into his consulting room and shuts himself in again, perhaps in order to rest. In any case, if I think about him too, Father is now all by himself.

Then, instead of playing in the yard, I sat still on the sofa and, while this day's clouds were passing over our last walnut tree, closed my eyes. And without my eyes I saw the clouds, as if they were passing inside me. And under these clouds, I first thought a little about Herr Magirius and then longer about Herr Veilchenfeld, whom I knew much better, and I wondered whether they would be put side by side in their coffins, since Herr Magirius was also *without connections*. And he was so closely trusted with the work of our philosopher that he could have devoured it, Father says. He then asks me if I wouldn't feel like driving with him to Frohna to pick up eggs at Herr Verhören's, but I don't feel like it and I stay on the sofa and close my eyes again and prefer to imagine.

How Dr Magirius, standing in the shadow of a house wall, introduces us to Herr Veilchenfeld, who has not yet been with us very long.

And this is Professor Veilchenfeld of Leipzig University, of whom you have certainly heard, says Herr Magirius, as he introduces him to us.

Pleased to meet you, says Father to Herr Veilchenfeld.

Pleased to meet you, says Herr Veilchenfeld to Father.

And we bow too and look up at Herr Veilchenfeld, who, in addition to his black hat, wears an enormous fleece coat much too warm for this time of year. But under the fleece coat, as everyone knows who has seen Herr Veilchenfeld at some time in a jacket or a shirt, or has been startled by him out walking, he is thin and delicate, because everything about him—head, hat, feet, fingers—is tender and fragile. Yes, there is less and less of me, Herr Veilchenfeld often says and smiles and tugs at his coat. Soon I will surely disappear completely, he says and laughs, and we drive him through town in our ailing car to the stone quarry, and so to our house.

First Herr Veilchenfeld sits by Father, then, because he's not enough weight on the front axle, he moves to us in the back. And he says he has not been among people for an eternity.

Do you know how long an eternity is? Herr Veilchenfeld asks me.

No, I say.

It is long, he says, very long. And he tells us how lately,

instead of talking to him, people hurry by him silently, and in telling us, he becomes completely agitated. We can smell the agitation. And sometimes he says to Father *Doctor* and then again *My dear sir*, while Father sometimes says *Professor* and sometimes *Dear professor*. And because he hasn't spoken with people for such a long time, he even makes mistakes in speaking, slips of the tongue all the time. Despite that, Herr Veilchenfeld is glad to be among people, and he's glad to talk to them, too. Who knows whether I could still hold my own at all in human society, says Herr Veilchenfeld. Meanwhile, the heavier Dr Magirius, who lectured from the works of Herr Veilchenfeld years ago in the larger cities of Asia Minor, and as a result caught one of those illnesses that sneaks up from behind, now sits beside Father and weighs down the axle quite well.

Well then, let's talk, says Herr Veilchenfeld time and again, and looks from one to the other.

But we are all silent.

Then we won't talk? asks Herr Veilchenfeld.

And we continue to be silent.

Then because this evening there is nothing else on his mind—this has emerged little by little—during the drive Herr Veilchenfeld already tries to acquaint Father with the most important features of his philosophy: what kind of philosophy it is and what it isn't and also what it never can be. Yes, he even describes the table where he wrote it. In doing so he has to bend far forward in the narrow car in order to be heard clearly. Now, Father is listening to him, of course, only he has difficulty with the strange words which Herr Veilchenfeld, in the rear seat, sticks into his sentences. For Father studied something very different from what Herr

Veilchenfeld did, and even that was a long time ago. And Father has not had the chance to read a real book for so long! He is completely taken up by the office hours during the day and the perpetual night bell. And then Father has actually even extended his practice in recent years. Whereas before he only treated patients in our town, now he drives out as far as Mittweida and Russdorf and treats them there, too. On top of that, the pains in his leg, which he can't soothe himself because the leg isn't there any more, as it's now wooden. A Frenchman sits in there and stabs me with a knife all the time, says Father. There. And he knocks on it. And now he has to pay attention to the road; there's fog that he must drive the car through safely. Despite that, he nods his head continually, but no, he can't really answer Herr Veilchenfeld. And Herr Magirius, to whom the philosophical expressions are naturally all familiar, and who could have easily turned around and answered, Herr Magirius is not himself this evening. His illness is back again. He had hardly sat down beside Father before he fell asleep, which is his illness. Again and again Herr Veilchenfeld has to pluck at his shoulder and repeat his question, and Herr Magirius always slumps, and time and again the answer fails to come. So that after many disappointments, Herr Veilchenfeld breaks off the explanation of his philosophy and turns to us and asks me what my favourite subject at school is and what meal...

Drawing and macaroni, I say.

Aha, Herr Veilchenfeld says, and pulls a sugar cube out of his pocket for my sister and me. But we may not bite it because that's bad for our teeth. We must let it melt in our mouths and suck the sugar water, so that it can be absorbed slowly into our blood. Herr Veilchenfeld also strokes the back of my head, which he says is *artistic*. And so on through our twilit little town, hidden in fog, until our house, which stands somewhat beyond, on the other side of the stone quarry, so that Herr Veilchenfeld, Father says, can get out without being afraid and stretch and move around outside the car a little, because here no one sees him. So while Father rouses Herr Magirius, we take Herr Veilchenfeld between us and lead him to our house. Mother comes to meet us at the entrance. Herr Veilchenfeld kisses her hand and straight away thanks her for the invitation.

You have invited me, he exclaims again and again.

But of course, Mother says.

Well, says Herr Veilchenfeld, well. And because he has said nothing for so long, he can't find the words that he wants to say. They are here, Herr Veilchenfeld says and indicates his tongue, but it will take a while until I . . .

Come in, Mother says, after she has waited long enough and the words have not come.

At all events I shall never forget this invitation, even if I should live to be one hundred years old, which, however, I hold to be improbable, Herr Veilchenfeld says.

Then because he is still shy with us, we take him between us again and lead him into the big room on the ground floor, where Grandfather died after a long difficult illness, and Mother has already heated the room and opened and set the table. She's even put a vase with some flowers on it. Herr Veilchenfeld, as our most important guest, has to sit at the head of the table, where he exclaims again and again how long it's been since he has been among people. But what do you want, he says, that's the way it is in our time. It isn't true that history can teach nothing; it is merely that there are no students.

Mother has not made any special fuss with the meal, but instead cooked quite a usual supper in her cold and high-ceilinged kitchen. She brings the soup to the table in a pot, in order to serve it around from above our heads. The bread is placed in a basket; everyone takes what he wants to eat. Finally she serves a stew in the big Jena glass bowl. She doesn't tell us what it's called, but there seem to be noodles in it. Herr Veilchenfeld praises her meal from the first spoonful of soup. And, after he has begged Mother for permission, he breaks bread into it in little pieces. Again and again he gazes around the room; it is strange to him, and its corners are still completely unexamined by him. He seems to be entirely carried away by his feelings, there in his black dress suit which he hasn't worn for a long time because he doesn't dine out any more. The entire time he wants to inform us of something, since in recent years he has indeed written some *for later*, but *owing to a lack of social environment*, he hasn't been speaking any more. He wants to, as he says, take us into his confidence, but the necessary words don't come to him, or he gets befuddled (he says: *febuddled*). Upset, bent over his plate, spoon in hand, he sits there and keeps opening his mouth, but nothing comes out. Meanwhile the good stew that Mother has cooked steams in his face, so that drops of sweat run down his cheeks, which he has to wipe away with the back of his hand so that they don't fall into the plate. Till I notice all of a sudden that they're not drops of sweat at all, but tears. Herr Veilchenfeld is actually sitting there and crying into his soup!

But Herr Veilchenfeld, you really don't have to upset yourself so, Mother says and shakes a warning finger at him. Tell us instead: How did you spend the winter?

Oh, just somehow or other, Herr Veilchenfeld says, and

he wants to say something more, but nothing further comes.

It goes without saying that we wanted to invite you, Mother says, and lays her hand on his arm. And it also won't be the last time. Right? she asks Father.

No, not the last time, says Father, who, having folded his hands in front of the good stew, at last would like to go on eating. We frequently invite people whom we don't know very well. And then Herr Veilchenfeld studied in Leipzig, just like Father, even though in another *guild*, Father says. And now eat, dear Veilchenfeld, he says, everything is getting cold. And then in order to give him an appetite, he even lists what besides the noodles Mother put in the food, but Herr Veilchenfeld simply can't eat. Nearly all his former colleagues and acquaintances have broken off contact with him; I am completely alone, he says. After over forty shared years, no one knows him any more. His students—and he has indeed had hundreds of students—have *written him off*. When he calls them, they are not at home; when he writes to them, they don't write back. And whereas the people in our town had always greeted him, as long as they hadn't known who he was, since they have known *from which corner he comes,* they have stopped too. Now they behave as if he doesn't exist, as if he's not in the same world. Of course a relationship with books replaces that with people, but only to a certain degree. Doesn't it? asks Herr Veilchenfeld. Then he gets up and goes to the window and looks at the vegetable garden.

Are you looking for something? asks Mother.

Oh, says Herr Veilchenfeld, so what should I be looking for?

And don't you want to eat any more? asks Mother.

Oh, says Herr Veilchenfeld, I would certainly like to eat.

Then sit down, take your spoon, and continue eating, dear Herr Veilchenfeld, Mother says and points to his chair. Father also points to his chair, and my little sister too.

Do you have beans in the garden? Herr Veilchenfeld asks Mother.

No, we don't have any beans this year, Mother says to Herr Veilchenfeld.

And tomatoes? asks Herr Veilchenfeld.

No, Mother says, no tomatoes either.

Curious, when I would be so glad to talk to people and would so gladly correct their misunderstandings, says Herr Veilchenfeld, when he has sat down again. But he may not, he ...

And now let's all eat, says Father.

At one point while he was at our house, Herr Veilchenfeld resolved always to be on his guard and not to lose his nerve. I am not always on my guard, however, he says, and I lose my nerve sometimes anyway.

Father fills Herr Veilchenfeld's glass; Herr Magirius will be asleep again quite soon; Mother, when she drinks, drinks quietly; my sister makes noises while doing so.

Gretel, Mother says.

Yes, she says.

Control yourself, says Mother.

Then Herr Veilchenfeld wants to show us a picture of his wife (who has already been dead now for seventeen years) when she was still alive, only he doesn't have the picture with him, but instead it's in the other jacket, in the one hanging in the wardrobe at home.

No, Herr Magirius wants nothing more, neither to eat nor to drink. I look at Herr Veilchenfeld. I think, now he's going to lose his nerve, but he doesn't lose it again after all. Then I look at his hands, his jacket, his jacket buttons. On one sleeve he has some, on the other not. My sister, when she drinks, is still making noises.

Margarete, Father has to say.

On the evening when Herr Veilchenfeld ate with us out of the Jena glass bowl, there was then still an apple for everyone, but Herr Veilchenfeld preferred to take his home with him and to eat it later, before going to sleep. After he had neatly folded his napkin, Mother sent him with Herr Magirius over to the armchairs by the fireplace, and everyone sat down in a chair while Father went to get the cigars from his consulting room.

It was strange that Herr Veilchenfeld, who had not been among people for so long, was now suddenly sitting in an armchair in our big ground-floor room.

Once Mother heard steps in the garden, but no doubt she was mistaken.

And now the philosophical discussion, to which all had looked forward, each for a different reason: Herr Magirius wanted to quickly get to know another side of Father, who as his doctor was soon to write out his death certificate; Father wanted to finally hear Herr Veilchenfeld's philosophy from his own mouth for once, because he had always respected him, if only from a distance; and Herr Veilchenfeld, because he especially wanted to compose the words remaining to him into sentences once again around people and to hear himself talk. Whether Mother looked forward to the discussion I don't know; I can't say.

When one has not spoken at all for so long, despite a great compulsion to speak, says Herr Veilchenfeld, one would most like to use one's nails to scratch off oneself everything which has thus developed and matured in the course of time and fling it into one long sentence and wrap it around the unsuspecting audience. Hence, around you, he says. Surely you can see it yourselves, he says, and as a matter of fact we all see how he runs his scholarly fingers over his head. The question is merely, with which words one begins such a sentence, he says, and then doesn't start at all on his philosophy, which all of us are awaiting. Instead, he speaks about a long walk which he took around our town just after his move out to us. Little by little, from all sides, he saw our town lying before him. Like all little towns, it had rooted itself and withdrawn into one of the natural recesses of the area that seem created for it. In the foothills of the Hoher Hain, as it happened. Naturally, you must first clear your horizon of the various chimneys which always push themselves to the fore in such a panorama, so that the, the, the, Herr Veilchenfeld says, and he has forgotten the word. And he lets himself sink deeper in his armchair, so that his embarrassment can't be seen. Now Mother opens the window a little because it seems so stuffy to her, leans out a little, doesn't see much outside either, though, and comes back to us. Strange how often even the really simple words escape me, as just now the word "impression," which I obviously wanted to say, although I once knew *Faust* by heart—both versions— the three hundred most important poems of our classical writers, and the most interesting parts of Kant's *Critique*. Anyway, back to the walk, he announces. As you know, the history of mankind, which has always been closely tied to regions, also leads nowhere at all, as I have tirelessly demonstrated for thirty-five years, Herr Veilchenfeld continues. Yet people say: But nonetheless! instead of listening to me. In any case, I'd gone then, as I recall, through the Schrannen Gate and outside the town. Anyway, then when I came back, the town was completely changed, and I was no longer myself. Now you will naturally say to yourselves: Something must have happened. At any rate, Herr Veilchenfeld recounted, because I had resolved upon a long march, a comprehensive course of inquiry into my new environment, I had packed myself some bread and butter. The bread and butter was wrapped in a piece of paper and stuck in my jacket pocket, where I felt it while walking. I had laced boots on my feet, a bamboo walking stick in my hands, over my head a dappled blue autumn sky, and in my head the central question, not just for me but for our entire species. For although the question was solved long ago—by me, among others—our need to see a fulfilment in history is still very powerful. And to look upon oneself, one's nation, one's culture, and the various regions in which all this has developed, as swiftly disappearing, accidental, and insignificant—that courage is given to extremely few, especially on such vast and extensive days, when everything wants to immortalise itself and open itself before one, as though it were real. Now, says Herr Veilchenfeld, if I were younger, I don't want to say how young, I don't want to say how much younger, just younger in general, because in reality of course I ... perhaps if one also doesn't examine me closely ... but for a long time, internally, the age of the tortoise of Tierra del Fuego, of the voracious crocodile ...

Well, as for this walk, Herr Veilchenfeld says, and Mother comes with the coffee and places it on the low Turkish table in front of Herr Veilchenfeld and Herr Magirius and Father. In any case, I had the impression that in this part of the world not only death, but also life, is allowed, he says. And so I go by the Schrannen House with keen steps—now listen carefully—and out of town, and I make note of a few aphorisms—and I must have somehow gone astray or gotten stuck or lost myself in the landscape or in my thoughts, because suddenly I'm standing in front of a building that doesn't fit in this piece of land, as it seems to me. Need I say that I considered this building to be uninhabited and uninhabitable? Then I thought of a prison. The walls were thick, there were grates over the windows, there was a flag hanging on the roof. Do you know the feeling of losing yourself? Herr Veilchenfeld asks Father. Do you also lose yourself sometimes?

Without a doubt, Father says, stroking his beard.

In the landscape or in your thoughts?

In both, now and then, says Father.

Indeed, says Herr Veilchenfeld. The strength needed even just to cross the street, the strength to keep to something. And he studies Father for a long time. And Father, who knows what Herr Veilchenfeld means, nods but says nothing, because he hopes Herr Veilchenfeld will come back to his philosophy all the more quickly. Instead, Herr Veilchenfeld cites or makes up the sentence about how life comes from the abyss and drags on for a while, and then retreats back into the abyss without trace or consequence. Herr Magirius nods and has Father give him a light once again, because his cigar, although he rolled it between his palms for such a long time, won't draw. But hardly has Father lit it and hardly has my little sister settled in on Father's good leg, because she does not care about ideas yet, and hardly has Mother poured the coffee into the cups, when we hear steps in the yard, voices and ... Sometimes when she lifts her finger in the air and she is the only one of us to hear something on the stairs or behind a door or in the yard, Mother is exactly right after all, Father once said.

Someone is there. Turn off the light, Father calls to me through the big room. Because of his leg, he doesn't get up very quickly. But before I can run to the switch and turn off the light, we hear a pane tinkle in my parents' bedroom, and then another, and out behind our elderberry bush someone shouts: Get Veilchenfeld out of here, or there's going to be trouble!

They have come on my account. I had thought that they would come, Herr Veilchenfeld says almost cheerfully, and stands up.

But how do they know that you're here? exclaims Father, who likewise stands up and carefully lays my sister, who is still sleeping, in his warm armchair.

Oh, they know everything, Herr Veilchenfeld says and smiles.

Now, exclaims Father, I am not prepared to let this scum, who spread themselves out in front of our houses and who ...

Call the police, Mother says to Father. But Father shakes his head. Then he goes through the room and into the hall to the front door and places his hand on the handle and now is about to open the door and rush out.

Stay here, cries Mother. Please.

Whether, if Mother had not cried out and held him by the sleeve, Father actually would have rushed into the yard at this moment, I don't know.

It would indeed be better if I were to leave now and set forth my thoughts, which are in any case muddled, another time. Otherwise they really will wreck everything here for you, Herr Veilchenfeld says to Father, and gestures toward our nice, intact, though now also dark, room. Then he takes his apple from the mantelpiece and is on the point of going into the hall, where his fleece coat and his hat are hanging. Dr Magirius, who has become quite pale, also wishes to go into the hall.

And the coffee, Mother calls suddenly, and points to the Turkish table, where the coffee is standing.

Ah yes, says Herr Veilchenfeld.

All remain standing and turn around and go to the Turkish table and pick up their cups, although no one knows exactly whether he has taken the right cup and not one of the others. The cups are hot and they're steaming. Herr Veilchenfeld and Herr Magirius put their cups to their lips immediately, in order to finish quickly, and Herr Magirius succeeds as well, but Herr Veilchenfeld does not succeed. Perhaps his coffee is hotter than Herr Magirius', or Herr Veilchenfeld cannot stand hot things, or he is so flustered that he can't concentrate on drinking, or his throat has shut.

You don't have to drink the coffee if you can't, Herr Veilchenfeld, exclaims Mother as she sees how difficult it will be for Herr Veilchenfeld to drink his coffee.

No, Herr Veilchenfeld says. You have made the coffee, and now I will drink it.

But when I made the coffee, we couldn't have anticipated this at all, Mother says, and points toward the yard.

No, Herr Veilchenfeld says. Now it will be drunk.

And he holds the cup in his hands and blows into it.

Careful, you'll splash yourself, Mother exclaims, because

in blowing Herr Veilchenfeld is splashing. He has already splashed his hands and his sleeves and his thick coat.

Hot, he says over and over, hot. And even though he blows on it, he simply can't drink his coffee, although Herr Magirius has long finished his coffee.

Come, Veilchenfeld, my wife will make you a new cup next time, Father calls from the hall. He was the first to realise that Herr Veilchenfeld would not be able to drink his coffee and he wants something to happen.

It is inexplicable to me, but I don't seem to be able to drink the coffee at the moment, Herr Veilchenfeld says and shakes his head at himself and places his cup back on the table. Maybe his throat really is shut.

Yes, put it down and come, Father calls to Herr Veilchenfeld through the door.

Yes, I would like to go too, says Herr Magirius, although his cigar is drawing well now, and he doesn't know where to put it, because he doesn't want to take it with him into the yard. But then he finds an ashtray and puts it in there. Then he buttons his coat closed. Father too, who this evening makes much more noise than usual with his artificial leg, flings his jacket on and puts on his doctor's hat, so that he finally looks like a proper small-town doctor again.

Are you leaving too? Mother asks Father.

I'm not afraid, I say.

My sister, who has just woken up, isn't afraid either.

Wherever I go, I bring misfortune in the form of brutal violence, Herr Veilchenfeld says to Father. I carry misfortune, like black birds on both my shoulders.

Yes, perhaps you should really keep out of the way during the next few days, says Father to Herr Veilchenfeld. That can only help.

They're behind the house, Herr Magirius says.

May I come with you? I ask Father. I'd like to.

No, says Father. You look after your mother.

And why don't you call the police? Mother asks Father. Supposedly we have police.

No! exclaims Herr Veilchenfeld. For God's sake not the police.

And why must he keep out of their way? I ask Father. What has he done, then?

The debased life in all its grandeur, emerging from the depths, which you in your thinking do not sufficiently take into account, Herr Magirius says to Herr Veilchenfeld, is now roaming through our gardens and smashing our windows.

Soon to disappear into the inferno, Father says.

Let's hope so, says Mother.

And how should I look after her? I ask Father.

Who should he look after? my sister asks Mother.

If you ask me, they are now nearby, reassembling for a second attack, Herr Magirius says to Herr Veilchenfeld.

Oh, you protect her from the rowdies who made that noise just now and threw something, Father says to me and grabs his car key. Suddenly he's speaking very loudly. Then from the hall Father turns on the light in front of the garage, so that he can already see from the door who is there and how many, and in the hall he can consider what he will say to them.

Why are you speaking so loudly? my sister asks Father.

I'm not speaking loudly at all, says Father to my sister.

And to Herr Veilchenfeld, Father says: I'm very sorry, my dear Veilchenfeld, but I think I should drive you back now.

And why did they throw something? I ask Father.

Who threw something? asks my sister.

No one threw anything, Mother says to my sister.

But it's not at all necessary for you to drive me back. I can manage this short stretch on foot quite easily, Herr Veilchenfeld says to Father, and he sticks his apple in his fleece coat. I am not timid by nature, and they haven't intimidated me either.

All the same, I'd prefer to drive you back, says Father to Herr Veilchenfeld.

But I don't wish to drag you into this business by having you drive me somewhere, Doctor, Herr Veilchenfeld says, and seizes Father by his jacket sleeve.

Yes, it would be nice, really, if there were a man in the house, says Mother, who can in fact put up with Herr Veilchenfeld well, but is not willing to be alone in the house when someone is prowling around.

But I will be right back, Father says to Mother and strokes her hair. Then he presses down the door handle, pushes open the front door with his good leg, and steps hastily into the yard, to find out at last who threw the stone. In addition to his torch, he's taken his walking stick, which is oak and usually hangs behind the front door, with him. Father can't take his war revolver with him because he has sworn never to touch a weapon again. That's why he buried it in the woods and has forgotten where.

You stay here, he says to me.

And he limps out and calls into the darkness: Is there anyone here? Is there anyone here? And he shines his torch over the yard and the bushes and the garage, but the ones who threw something don't answer him. Then Father even goes behind the house; we can hear him pull his artificial leg along the garden path. Is there anyone here? he calls.

Come back, Mother calls out into the yard. Don't leave us here alone.

No foolishness, Doctor, Herr Veilchenfeld calls.

Think about your family, calls Herr Magirius.

But I'll come right back, Father calls from behind the house. We no longer see him. We stand in the hall and hold our breath and look out into the darkness. Because Father is outside, Mother's eyes move rapidly to and fro.

It was probably only a very small stone that they threw, Herr Veilchenfeld says to calm Mother.

A *colloquium interruptum,* Herr Magirius says to Herr Veilchenfeld, and gives a short laugh.

A warning, so that I know how far I may go, Herr Veilchenfeld says to us. Good, I have been warned. This time I have gone too far; that I know. From now on I won't go so far any more. I will stay at home.

Such a thing shouldn't be possible, neither here nor anywhere else, Mother says to Herr Veilchenfeld.

Is there anyone here? Is there anyone here? Father calls from behind the house. His voice can be heard as far as the stone quarry, only nobody answers him. Either they've run away, or they're standing behind the shed. But Father doesn't go behind the shed because there's no more path there. Instead he comes back.

Come, Veilchenfeld, they've gone away, Father says and catches hold of Herr Veilchenfeld in order to secure him, although usually on account of his leg Father himself always links arms with Mother or leans against her. Now Herr Magirius comes also and takes hold of Herr Veilchenfeld on the other side, although he too has difficulties with his legs. Nevertheless, they try to form a group and to walk in step. And they take Herr Veilchenfeld to the car safely, and Father first pushes Herr Veilchenfeld in, and then Herr Magirius, and rolls the car out of the yard without turning on the headlights, and then drives away fast. Meanwhile, along with Mother I lock the front door and carry my little sister, who's fallen asleep again on Father's armchair, upstairs. In my parents' bedroom I sweep up the pieces of glass and stop up the holes with newspapers and look after Mother, who keeps wanting to lean out of the window and gaze after Father.

No, I say, you mustn't do that! and I pull her away from the window. Then Father comes and I lie down and at once I have to...

If you consider that Herr Veilchenfeld is already over sixty and isn't the healthiest person either, says Father, who examined him one Monday morning in Heidenstrasse and diagnosed a bad heart and then prescribed little white pills, although they probably won't help him. If you consider...

Yes? I ask.

Instead of the sixty kilos Herr Veilchenfeld should weigh, he doesn't even weigh fifty and he keeps losing more and he will, despite the greatness of his mind, soon disappear and be rapidly forgotten.

And, I ask, if you consider this?

Exactly, Father says.

Mother lowered all the blinds so they couldn't throw anything through the windows again, and lay down in bed because of the shock and her colic, although she doesn't take anything at all, and Father gets his syringes and hurries upstairs to her again and again with them, while Aunt Ilse stands in the kitchen and has to cook for us. We stand around Aunt Ilse, but we aren't to tell her anything about the windows, because she could tell someone else, and that would just make everything worse, Father said.

And may we tell her that Herr Veilchenfeld was at our house? we ask.

No, not that either, Father says, by no means that. And he takes a syringe and hurries to Mother's room, where we hear her groaning, while Aunt Ilse calls from the kitchen that the meal is ready. After the meal, which Mother can't bear to smell, let alone eat, I go into town with my sister to see Herr Veilchenfeld through the window of his flat, but we don't see Herr Veilchenfeld, even though his light is on. On the way back we see his silhouette on the wallpapered wall. But it isn't only Herr Veilchenfeld's silhouette; we can hear him coughing. He seems to be sitting over his books at the table and to have fallen asleep or to be thinking of something outside himself, perhaps a new idea. He is bent far forward in order to press it out and immediately write it in a book, so that it's not lost. When we're back at home again and my sister is lying in bed and is probably already asleep, and Aunt Ilse has tidied up the kitchen or says she has and is gone again, and I'm alone with Father, I ask him if he was at Herr Veilchenfeld's and he says: I was, I was.

And?

They had spoken, not about the rowdies, but about Herr Veilchenfeld's heart, which is no longer beating correctly, as Father can hear clearly. And they had talked about me. I had pleased him, I had *my wits about me.*

And what else did he say, I asked.

Well, he had asked Father, did I really enjoy drawing so much. If so, he could give me drawing lessons once a week.

Can he draw then?

Well, if he wants to teach you, he certainly would be able to, says Father. And he buys me a box of coloured pencils and a stack of drawing paper behind my sister's back, because otherwise she would have demanded to have the same thing, and one Tuesday afternoon, with freshly washed hands, I cross the marketplace to draw with Herr Veilchenfeld.

Herr Veilchenfeld, Father says, can sit over a book all day and, connected through the book with centuries and millennia, he can *listen into* the past. He sits at his table, his hand on his forehead, squints into his room, leans forward, then back, then closes his eyes and hears the voices of the past, not with his ears, but with his head, each voice clearly distinguished from the others, entire choruses of the past, and, with his own silent voice, he calls through his study and into the corridor and out the open bedroom window and, at apple tree height, over his rear garden and our Amselgrund away into landscapes and times and he makes himself heard from his chair, with his slightly Saxon accent.

Yes, you must imagine it about like that, says Father. Whether Herr Veilchenfeld will be heard, no one can say yet, it's too early for that, he says, but he suspects that no, Herr Veilchenfeld will not be heard, his voice will perish. Sometimes—he does not always sleep well at night—he falls asleep hearing beautiful things, but he hears still more in his sleep. Herr Veilchenfeld was surprised, says Father, by his being able to hear in all directions, and at the window once, his cigar in his mouth, he called it *the Great Ear.*

He came through the corridor to me at the flat door and gave me his hand. He had on the same suit as when he was at our house, when he couldn't drink the coffee.

So you have found my cave, he asked me.

Oh, I said, you can be seen on the wall.

I can be seen from the street? Herr Veilchenfeld asked, and he turned a little pale.

Yes, I said, your shadow.

So have you identified my cave by my shadow? asked Herr Veilchenfeld, who hadn't known at all that his shadow could be seen from below.

Yes.

Then Herr Veilchenfeld said that the shadows of philosophers are their books. I would probably want to see them, too. Or not? Herr Veilchenfeld asked me.

That would be really nice, I said.

Apart from Father, Herr Magirius and the cleaning lady, I was the first to enter his flat and be allowed to *look around* it. I looked around first in the corridor, then in his study. I could see the back garden through a little window in the corridor. I saw the old beanpoles that he walked around and that he always straightened out because of his love of order.

The feeling that I was about to suffocate, which I had when I entered his flat, now faded. Instead I now had the feeling that it was probably too warm for me at Herr Veilchenfeld's. I took off my jacket and hung it on a hook, and he took me by the arm and led me into his study, which he called his *cabinet*. He called the door *the door to my cabinet* and the window *my cabinet window*. Then I went to the bay corner, which until then I had always just imagined and that extended into the street. Here and in the middle of the room were tables, both with polished tops. There were books lying on the one in the middle, some left open. The bay table was empty. First Herr Veilchenfeld led me to the table in the middle.

Here, in case you are interested, I have written some of my books, said Herr Veilchenfeld and rapped on the table top.

Oh really, I said.

Yes, earlier, said Herr Veilchenfeld. Not all of them, naturally, and also not the most important. They were engendered before and at other tables, in other rooms, when my wife was still alive and I still had more book courage. But those tables and those rooms I cannot show you any more, they lie far behind me, perhaps they no longer exist. Or other people live in them now, other people whom I don't know at all, and who don't know me either. It is, said Herr Veilchenfeld, as if I had never been in those rooms.

Oh, I said, surely there's still someone who remembers you.

And who or what should remember me, asked Herr Veilchenfeld. The walls? The floor? The door?

Not the door, more likely the walls, I said and knocked on the cabinet wall.

Because of the many books that were in the room, it was just as cramped as I had always imagined from the street. No, more cramped. It also smelled, as I had always thought. Herr Veilchenfeld, who when he was writing had to breath in and out a lot, should have aired the room more often. In one corner there stood a climbing plant that was withering and should have been thrown away, but Herr Veilchenfeld had probably not yet noticed it at all. Or he was so alone in the cabinet that it didn't matter to him what stood beside him, or he didn't know where he should throw it away. The cabinet floor was covered with a carpet. Along the wall was a sofa.

So your father let you come to me then, said Herr Veilchenfeld. I must say, that surprises me.

Why? I asked.

Well, anyway, said Herr Veilchenfeld. And he got two leather-covered chairs from the next room. I had to choose one. Sit properly on the seat, not just on the edge, otherwise you might possibly break the chair for me, said Herr Veilchenfeld. You're not afraid of me, are you, of such an old man?

Oh, I said, you're not all that old.

What am I then?

Oh, you're at the nicest age.

Do you really mean that, or have you read that somewhere? I really mean it.

Well then, said Herr Veilchenfeld.

His hands shook as he laid a portfolio with drawings on the bay table, but he didn't let anything fall yet. It would take another couple of years until he was letting everything fall. I opened my box with the new pencils and laid my drawing paper on the table, and Herr Veilchenfeld told me how much trembling and sweating had already taken place on the chairs we were sitting on just then. They were actually examination chairs.

I always demanded a great deal from my students and was always a person to be respected, which, as you see me now, you probably cannot imagine, said Herr Veilchenfeld and pointed down at himself. The error does not lie here.

What error? I asked.

Sometimes I have actually wondered if I do not only have myself to blame.

How's that?

Yes, you might think that I have always laid a ruler beside me and beat the world of ideas into them with it, but that's not true, said Herr Veilchenfeld. Learning, I have always said to myself, must be fun. Did you know that already?

No.

Well, said Herr Veilchenfeld, now you know it.

Then he opened up his portfolio with drawings and watercolours, which he mostly drew or collected during the holidays, and I had to sit right next to him and look at them and tell him which of them I was struck by and why I considered them good or bad or middling. They looked to me like landscapes, trees, hills, gates, lanes or ruins, but also some people's faces were among them, faces he had seen one day when he was much younger, and held on to, he said.

I told him which I liked and which I didn't, but I couldn't say why.

Yes, he said, we still must learn the reasons.

There were also drawings and paintings, with and without frames, on Herr Veilchenfeld's bookshelves and hanging on his window wall, which because of the long time that had passed since their creation, were completely yellowed or had mildew stains.

Every drawing has its history, said Herr Veilchenfeld, which of course is also recorded. If you knew in what sequence all of this has come into being, you would surely also say that what I did at the beginning was the most successful. That has to do with the courage that one has at the beginning. The older one then becomes, the less courage one has and also the less one succeeds. There, he said and pushed over to me a really ugly drawing of a mutilated man in a desert landscape who held a thin, almost transparent child pressed against him, as if he wanted to strangle him.

Yes, this is really ugly, I said, when did you draw it?

Last week, there, at this table, Herr Veilchenfeld said, and pointed to the middle table, but at night. Then he quickly put it away again.

So is that because now you don't have courage any more?
Yes, of course, he said.

At dawn, when Herr Veilchenfeld steps into the garden in
order to get his blood going, the grass he steps on is dew-
covered; his trousers, instead of being nicely fitted, are wrin-
kled and hang on him; his heart beats very quickly, as always
at this hour; his eyes are red from lying down; the sky above
him has not yet arched and pressed on his skull and will
soon have to decide in which colour it wants to show itself.
Herr Veilchenfeld squints when he sees the contents of his
garden under this sky, and with the help of memory he brings
it into the old alignment, with everything in its place. Then
he begins to draw the beanpoles into his circle. This is why it
happens that Herr Veilchenfeld has such wet shoes when he
goes to his writing desk. In town he is now called *the Violet,*
his house *the Violet House*, his walk *the Violet Walk*, and when
he passes by someone, *the Violet Smell*, and so on. He said
once: In the human head, even in the modern one, everything,
the most dangerous nonsense, is stirred in. After some time
everything is accepted as natural, like shrubs and flowers.

When I was with him for drawing, he put a flat cap on
to protect his head from the daylight or from the air or from
my view, laid his hands in front of himself on the table and
said: Well now, well now. Then he began the lesson. From
scratch, where one should always begin the lesson, he said,
and he explained which pencil and chalk and pen are used
in drawing, and made a connection between intention and

*Veilchenfeld: field of violets

media. During the explanation he became calmer and used to speaking and found many words again that had long been lost. Herr Veilchenfeld also became used to me, as I became used to him. At the end, when I had yawned a couple of times, he brought a bowl with biscuits from the kitchen and pushed them over to me, but I didn't take any because they had probably been standing around for a long time and had become completely stale.

The time when I was at Herr Veilchenfeld's, he had probably moved the table into the bay, so that he got light from three sides through the bay windows. He didn't see very well any more. But now, when he raised his head, he could see a part of our town lying below. Only seldom can you see into the courtyards of a town at an angle from above. I saw a lot that I would have liked to draw, if I had only been more able. But Herr Veilchenfeld not only drew at the bay table, he wrote at the bay table too. What he had written he laid on the table in the middle, so that when you entered his cabinet, you saw at once how much was already completed. While writing he was alone and with the other person at the same time. And he saw his fellow citizens who would have preferred to chase him away—out of fear, said Father, they were afraid of him!—first up Heidenstrasse and then down again, with and without their heads covered. He saw others in front of the Höhlers' fence, how they chatted together and looked up at him and laughed or spat on the ground. In his bay he could imagine, like all philosophers, that he stood or sat over them and looked down at them from above and perfectly studied their gestures. And yet, said Father, he is not arrogant, but rather knows that, in philosophising, one is not above the people, but rather stands at their side.

Reality as gruesome rumour, which goes around our town, Father says to Mother, when I tell them what Frau Schellenbaum said in the dairy shop. She says in our Town Hall there is a cellar in which certain people are locked up and beaten, *so that they are out of circulation*. Sometimes at night, when she can't sleep, she can hear them crying out. Then she gets up, goes to the window, opens the window, but she sees nothing; she can only hear the cries.

No one is jailed on suspicion here, says Frau Übeleis, and pours milk into the pitcher for us.

Well, says Frau Schellenbaum, maybe I'm mistaken, maybe I'm just imagining it.

Anything so terrible shouldn't be imagined, says Frau Übeleis, and Frau Schellenbaum says: God knows it shouldn't! and we say goodbye and leave with the milk.

Because of the furniture and the books and the instruments, if he were not so slight, Herr Veilchenfeld could not move at all in his cabinet; as it is, he can, but only a little. A violin lay on a chair, which he carefully went around. Notes lay here and there on the floor, which he walked over when he had to go to the toilet one time that day. Probably the chest was also stuffed full of notes; there were some hanging out of the drawers. At one time Herr Veilchenfeld had had these notes all in his head, as he hastily told me, but those were other times. Back then not only his head, but his entire person, was filled with music—could be filled with music.

That had been during his studies in Leipzig; he had lived in Grimmschenstrasse there, above a music shop. And since by virtue of his address he was already completely musical, he went, no, flew, through the broad streets of Leipzig utterly elated. And every week he played music with three friends, who are now all dead (or as good as dead), mostly at his place, because he had the largest room and the most lenient landlords. All night long they sat there with their instruments and went from playing one composer to another, wide awake even after midnight. And because I had drawn enough for that day, Herr Veilchenfeld led me to a shelf on which was fastened an old photograph of four young men, who sat with stringed instruments on their knees and looked at the camera. They were actually smiling, but looked stressed by all the music, if not shocked.

That was us, said Herr Veilchenfeld and pointed to the photograph.

Aha, I said, and was a little shocked myself, because Herr Veilchenfeld looked completely different now.

You don't recognise me? he asked me.

No, I said. For actually he had changed so much that he could have been any of the four, or in fact none of them.

There, said Herr Veilchenfeld. That's me, look! and pointed, as if randomly, to one.

Yes, I said, you can see it right away.

Herr Veilchenfeld pointed at his books, too, which had been placed on simple boards against the wall up to the ceiling and had seldom been dusted, as he also explained to me. Those I wrote myself, he said, and pointed to a shelf.

The whole shelf?

Yes.

And what are they about?

Oh, about everything, Herr Veilchenfeld said, and made an apologetic gesture.

About everything or about everything possible? I asked, but that he didn't tell me. Instead, he pulled out one of the books and put it in my hand, so that I could see how thick it was and how many pages the individual chapters had. I read a couple of the headings but I didn't understand them. When you consider how many people there are or once were who all could have written something down and left it behind, it seems to me that Herr Veilchenfeld had written disproportionately many books. Well, he had as many thoughts, and gladly wrote them down. Then Herr Veilchenfeld took the book back from me and put it in its place and quickly explained the others to me, too. There are the difficult ones, there the plain ones and there the scary ones, he said.

And which have you read?

All, said Herr Veilchenfeld, and pushed me toward the door.

Because it's such a nice Sunday morning, there go Father with Mother and Herr Laube the optician and Frau Laube, over to the Great Pond, on which the sun is glistening. They speak quietly about everything and don't notice that we are walking behind them and hear almost everything. That last night something happened here—what, I don't understand for a long time. It's not that I don't hear their sentences, I simply don't grasp their meaning.

It's certain that it hasn't rained around here for many days already, although there is something hanging in the sky that ought to split open, says Father. It happened in this weather. Father says: *the assault*, Mother: *the infamous action,* Herr

Laube: *an act of rage,* which he has long seen coming. While Frau Laube held her head again and again—she did it in front of Father and Mother—and simply did not want to believe it, because she thought such things do not happen, at least not around where we live. In short: It was during one of those nights that are made for such attacks, said Father, who as a doctor now has much to do—with his breath he must resuscitate the people who in the heat are falling like flies, and restore them to life. Of course, the days are still worse; the crickets—my sister says: the chirpers—clamour non-stop, and our market place with its bumpy paving stones, where all the streets run together, can hardly be crossed because of the heat. One would rather put a damp cloth on one's head and creep along by the houses, even if it means a detour. Naturally, such heat has an effect well into the night. At nine our light was turned off, then we went to sleep right away. When we woke up everything, apart from the smell, was already finished. It concerned Herr Veilchenfeld, in his shirtsleeves, without hat or tie. For him, after writing all through a hot day—his *Overworld*, his work!—exercising in the garden was not enough and in order to move around somewhat more, he wanted to go into town.

So imprudently, he actually went there, around eleven, says Mother.

No, exclaims Frau Laube, it was after midnight.

Let's say, said Father, before going to sleep.

So instead of lying down in bed, he wanted to go to the postbox quickly, because he'd written a letter to Switzerland that still had to be sent, said Frau Laube, and she heard it in the dairy shop, where for a week now nothing else has been spoken about. In any case, before or after midnight, Herr Veilchenfeld goes into town once again, where in between the *Casino* cinema and the *Lampenputzer* wine bar he comes upon the scene.

Why he goes by the *Lampenputzer* and not through Helenenstrasse, I don't understand. Doesn't he know, then, who patronises the *Lampenputzer*? Father says, and lights his pipe, which he has been slowly filling in his jacket pocket while he's been walking. If you look in his pockets, you will always find tobacco.

But the *Casino* is indeed much worse than the *Lampenputzer*. One should ask why he went by the *Casino*, not by the *Lampenputzer*, says Frau Laube, while Mother can see no difference between the *Lampenputzer* and the *Casino*.

Herr Laube has left the path in order to be nearer to where it is cool and, with his jacket over his arm, climbs through the yellow grass at the pond and lets the water slosh over his feet. He sees no difference and maintains it's all the fault of Herr Veilchenfeld. And he wonders if it was not even perhaps an unconscious provocation...

But my dear Laube, Father exclaims, how can you say such a thing. How can you...

All right, says Herr Laube, if you insist, I take back the word *provocation*. But at all events, in such weather and in his situation, to go to the *Lampenputzer* at night, what has become of healthy common sense? A place where, in such weather, one word indeed is enough to awaken the animal that sleeps in all of us, exclaims Laube the optician. If it then pounces, this animal, no one should be surprised. No, no, it was inexcusable for him to go to the *Lampenputzer*.

And to the *Casino*, adds Frau Laube, who is now walking next to her husband in the middle, while our father and our mother are separated from each other and walking on the sides. Now and then a green dragonfly comes and flies all around them.

In any case, Herr Veilchenfeld was on his way home and his letter was in the postbox, when he was *set upon* (Herr Laube), *attacked* (Mother), *kicked in the behind* (Father) the whole way down Turnvater-Jahn-Gasse, and finally *beaten up* under his own window by three or four young people who, as Mother says, stepped *tipsily* out of the cinema or, as Father says, out of the wine shop. With fists, as Mother says, while Father, early today, when he heard of the matter and immediately hurried to him, noticed under Herr Veilchenfeld's left ear traces of brass knuckles, because a punch doesn't look like *that*. At Herr Veilchenfeld's cry for help, several heads had indeed appeared in the windows in Jahn Gasse, but no one came down and intervened or even called out anything, but only watched. And, said Father, they had seen how the young people, among whom was also reportedly the grandson of the recently deceased former butcher Schmittchen (our greatest!), pounced on Herr Veilchenfeld. But they didn't just leave Herr Veilchenfeld lying in front of his house and clear off. Instead they grabbed him under his arms and dragged (Mother: *scraped*) him back along the whole of Turnvater-Jahn-Gasse and a part of Helenenstrasse and finally across our market, which was ghostly and still radiated heat, as far as the *Deutscher Peter*. Now the *Deutscher Peter* has long been one of our fashionable and most expensive restaurants, even if lately, because of the change of ownership, it's also a little run down.

We have never gone to the *Deutscher Peter*, says Father, and we never will go, either.

We too, says Frau Laube, only go to the *Deutscher Peter*

when we're invited, but who ever invites us to the *Deutscher Peter*? At the *Deutscher Peter* they pushed Herr Veilchenfeld, who at irregular intervals had been calling out for help through the entire town, through the courtyard entrance and into the separate assembly room, where he was awaited. Anyway, as he entered, because he *stumbled* (Mother), *greeted them* (Frau Laube), *was bleeding* (Father), he was received on all sides with hilarity. Here's the new delivery, they were saying. Herr Veilchenfeld said only: Gentlemen. Then he was silent. The assembly room guests, who were already drunk, shoved him against the diagonal wall of the assembly room and sat themselves down in their chairs in a semicircle around him, with their legs spread apart. They planted their legs on the right and left, so that they could have the chair backs in front of them. In this way they had encircled him (Frau Laube), reversed their roles (Herr Laube), mistreated him like a captured animal (Mother), tortured him (Father), and so on. Herr Veilchenfeld, except for: Gentlemen! had otherwise said nothing more, and the entire time only stared at the floor, which was soiled by beer puddles and strewn with sawdust. At most he now and then stroked his hair, which was still full and still his own, if of course also grey. In order to have real fun with him, they called him *Professor* and began a mock-philosophical discussion. So he was asked, for example, how much two plus two *really* is and if he can prove it. As he did not want to prove it, they threw lit matches at him and, in order to "extinguish" him, they doused him with the remains of the beer. Then the grandson of our former butcher danced around with him like a woman, cheek to shoulder. Finally, they forced him to drink a whole glass of beer, into which they had quickly slipped a couple of cigarettes, and to sing the song, "Hark, what enters from without."

But I cannot sing, Herr Veilchenfeld said. And beer doesn't agree with me, I am not accustomed to it.

What, they called out, you can't drink beer?

And Veilchenfeld, firmly: No.

Then the butcher's grandson went right up to Herr Veilchenfeld and took hold of his ear and said to him that he should be careful about how he expresses himself. They did not understand the word *no*, for example, as they were strange in that way.

But I really cannot tolerate beer, Herr Veilchenfeld said, I become nauseous from it, recounts Father.

But the one who was twisting his ear said: Come on, drink already, Violet.

And at least two of those in uniform who were present told Herr Veilchenfeld this was an official order and he had to finish the beer, Father says, while proceeding through the high grass. No wonder that, in the condition he was in after the beer, he confused the setting of the scene and he presumed he was in the public bar, not in the private assembly room of the *Deutscher Peter*. Again and again he said: Please, not so loud. Or: Please, you've had your fun with me, let me go home now. Until one explained to him—now we're coming to the high point of our walk, at the place where the bulrushes are—where he actually was. I see, Herr Veilchenfeld said.

Mother, we call from behind our parents.

Yes, says Mother, and she stops.

There's no need to be afraid, Professor, this is just between us, one of them said, Father tells Herr Laube and continues on.

Can we pick a couple of bulrushes, we ask Mother.

Bulrushes, Mother says, you want to go into the pond in your Sunday clothes?

Yes, we say, just one for each.

And possibly sink into this horrible mud before our eyes, says Mother.

Oh, I say, we won't sink.

In any case, Mother asks, you want to stick these reeking weeds in your face?

They don't reek, we call out, they smell good.

In any case, Father says, they now also stopped ...

In any case, Mother says, going into the pond is out of the question.

... and asked, says Father, whether it wouldn't suit him, if they were a little merry.

But if we can't get the bulrushes, the whole walk won't have been any fun, we call out.

I can't do anything about that, says Mother.

Let me go, please, Herr Veilchenfeld said, what more do you want from me, Father recounts to Herr Laube, am I not also a person?

All right, we say to Mother, then we're not going any farther, we'll sit here in the grass.

No, Mother says, you will not sit in the grass, you will go on nicely.

You heard what your mother says, Father says to us, well, then. But because he called himself a person, he says to Herr Laube, they did not leave him alone, and they asked each other whether Herr Veilchenfeld really was a person.

All right, I said, we'll come with you then.

Imagine that, said Frau Laube.

In any case, said Mother, you are not going into the pond.

And, said Father, to gain the proper perspective on whether Herr Veilchenfeld was a person, they began to examine him and to knock, especially on his head, because there it can be seen most readily, if someone is a person or not. And they took a string to measure . . .

Gretel, Mother calls, have I not forbidden . . .

Margarete, Father calls, and threatens her with his hand.

But I'm not going into the pond, my sister says.

. . . his head, Father says to Herr Laube, and takes his hand away again. Since for such a measurement they couldn't come close enough to his skull because of his hair, they had to cut it with a long paper scissors. In their grasp, it (the hair) bristled and stood on end in all directions. *That someone's hair is standing on end* is a phrase that one reads and hears over and over and that one can imagine, but now they could also see the phrase, so to speak, Father says to Herr Laube, on Herr Veilchenfeld in the *Deutscher Peter,* when he was touched. Suddenly the phrase about the hair stood physically and tangibly before them. Look how his hair is standing on end, isn't that magnificent, they called out, and they fetched still other guests from nearby who might find such a thing interesting. And they cut off Herr Veilchenfeld's hair that was standing on end until he was bald. In this condition they had let him go home; that's how the wife of Pietsch the stove maker came across him. She did not recognise him at first and couldn't even speak to him because she was so shocked by the sight of him, says Mother, when we are by the duck house, so right around the pond. Only much later, because Herr Veilchenfeld doesn't go on, but just keeps running his hand over his head again and again and supports himself against the wall of a house and has to cry, does she ask him something. She asks him whether he's *fallen* and hurt himself. Because she doesn't ask about his hair, in order not to embarrass him. Only with difficulty does she get Herr Veilchenfeld, whose entire body is trembling, to calm down somewhat.

Indeed he would like to be calm and simply to think away or to laugh off the incident, which Frau Pietsch does not want to judge. Again and again he makes jerky, fitful, sudden movements with his shoulders, such as Frau Pietsch has never seen before, and when he says something, he speaks so indistinctly that Frau Pietsch must repeatedly question him. She forgot straightaway most of what she had understood, or she didn't want to tell me it, Mother says to Father and to the Laubes. Anyhow, she then remembered that he said over and over: There, they befouled me, they defiled me! and pointed at his shirt and his trousers. But there was nothing to see, Frau Pietsch said and wanted to *brush him down*, but Herr Veilchenfeld had become completely numb and rigid and was wailing: Don't touch me, don't touch me! And when he was back at home, he spent the rest of the night burning everything he wore that they had thrown or doused or touched at the *Deutscher Peter*, in the kitchen oven. Where, because of the pressure, the fire did not catch, but only smouldered, so that by the end of the night a vast dark and foul-smelling smoke cloud, which came from his smouldering clothes, hung over Herr Veilchenfeld's house. At daybreak the vapours moved tediously and very low up Heidenstrasse and over the market and out to the Kellerwiese outside our town. Even at the present moment you can still smell the stench, so that Frau Laube asks: Will we ever be rid of it?

By evening, my dear Frau Laube, Father says reassuringly, everything will clear away.

Do you really think so, or do you merely hope so, Frau Laube asks Father.

I really think so, says Father.

Now we're on the stretch of shingle beach, which crunches under us, and Father and Mother and the Laubes are all silent.

Did they cut off all his hair, I ask and take hold of my hair.

Now look at that, says Mother and stands still, were you listening?

All then? I ask.

Yes.

And why did they cut it off?

Oh, says Mother and looks at Father first and then at the Laubes, but they don't know either or don't tell us. Oh, Mother says, they just did it.

And the police, I ask, they allow them to cut off his hair?

But then Mother and Father and Herr and Frau Laube only gave a quick laugh, and Herr Laube said that what happened with Herr Veilchenfeld's hair and nose and ears doesn't matter to the police. They don't interfere in such minor matters.

Why with his nose and his ears, I ask, because I completely missed Herr Veilchenfeld's nose and ears or I already forgot them again. Are his ears and his nose also ruined?

Yes, likewise, Herr Laube says, and we have been once around the pond.

Herr Veilchenfeld is one thing, the other thing is his work, Father says at breakfast, where there are poached eggs, because it's Sunday. Each of us gets one egg, only Father gets two, but he pushes the second aside, it goes back to the chickens. And indeed Herr Veilchenfeld's work is philosophical and pertains to the world in general. This work, at which Herr Veilchenfeld has been labouring for over thirty years, although it is not yet completely finished, is in all the libraries in the world. Where we live it is completely unknown, we have other concerns. Owing to the many ideas that Herr Veilchenfeld has crammed into the work, it is not at all so easy to understand, by God it isn't. I don't understand it at any rate, Mother says, when I ask her a question about the *Overworld* presented in the work. Because this world doesn't exist outside Herr Veilchenfeld's head, that's why I say *Overworld*, says Father. What one does not absolutely have to know, one can also live without knowing. After the death of Herr Veilchenfeld it will collapse anyway and will quickly be forgotten. Then the world will once again be as it was before Herr Veilchenfeld, without what he has put into it.

For a long time, our town talked about how Herr Veilchenfeld lost his hair. And just when they wish to forget about it again, Herr Veilchenfeld says to himself: I'll do it! and after lunch he goes into the police station, without taking off his hat, in order to lodge a complaint about the attack and to lodge the complaint against persons unknown with Herr Obermüller, who just now is on duty. But he does not accept it. Instead he says: Wait! and goes into the back room and doesn't return for a long time. Meanwhile his colleague Schaps cannot see Herr Veilchenfeld watching him work the whole time, and tells him, he should turn around and look at the wall, and he should also take his hat off. Then Herr Obermüller comes back and asks Herr Veilchenfeld if he has come *to lodge a complaint*. Yes, says Herr Veilchenfeld to his wall, I have been mistreated. So to lodge a complaint? Herr Obermüller asks again. Yes, says Herr Veilchenfeld. Then Herr Obermüller goes away again, and Herr Veilchenfeld stands in front of the wall. But then Herr Obermüller comes back with a sign that he hangs around Herr Veilchenfeld's neck. With this sign Herr Veilchenfeld is pushed out of the station into the street and must now walk through our town for two hours, but without his hat, says Herr Obermüller, who rides ahead of him on his bicycle. Many people walk behind and beside Herr Veilchenfeld. Others ride behind him on bicycles and ring their bells, to say nothing of the people who are watching out their windows. And Herr Obermüller rides along Helenenstrasse, where after the lunch break the shops are just opening again, then by Schrannen House and across the Schrannen Bridge, then he turns again and rides down Helenenstrasse again on the other side, where meanwhile, because news of Herr Veilchenfeld's "stroll" has quickly gotten around, many people have assembled, who all want to see him. Then they turn in the direction of the brick works, come past the train station and my school, where Herr Lohmann allows us all to step to the window, and finally to the market, through a dense crowd, who move back, laughing and appalled, and return to the police station. On the sign that he hung around his neck, Herr Obermüller has written: I will never again lodge a complaint with the police, "Professor" Bernhard Israel Veilchenfeld. The *never* is underlined. The people stand on the pavement or walk back and forth until dusk and hope that Herr Veilchenfeld will go through the town again, but he doesn't come out any more, instead he can go back home when it's dark. On the next day—a Saturday—we talk about him again, not just about his hair, but also about the injuries that he had on his face when he left the police station. And as it's a nice day again, we open the windows and tell each other across the street everything we know about the "stroll." Toward noon we go into town, and Mother, who wears a corset for her colic under her light summer dress and walks between Father and me, says that now he won't stay much longer.

After what they did with him yesterday that is not possible, instead Herr Veilchenfeld will now pack and go, she says.

Yes, says Father, if they let him.

Then we go back and forth for a while in front of the *Deutscher Peter* and we look through the window at the chairs, while others prefer to go back and forth in front of the police station, in order to look at everything there. (When we have not seen outrageous actions, we want at least to see the sites of the outrage, Father says.) Others, because it's Saturday, connect the useful with the pleasurable and go into the *Deutscher Peter* and have themselves served a beer at the bar and, because it's a nice day, come out again and blow the foam from their beer in the air or in the gutter. And glasses in hand, they look into the meeting room where Herr Veilchenfeld was shorn, and then with a turn of the head look over to the police station, where he wanted to lodge a complaint. And others, without beer, shuffle their feet and tell how long his "stroll" lasted and everywhere he was led past which buildings. Some have even come from the neighbouring villages and want to tell us everything, but we already know everything ourselves. That's why we go across the bumpy pavement to the other side of the market, from where we can see both the *Deutscher Peter* and the police station quite well, but we must not speak to anyone, that's what Mother would prefer. And we wonder whether something will happen again today, and we wait a long time for it, but on this Sunday morning nothing happens at first. Only that today our ice cream vendor Mausifalli is standing with his cart in front of the *Deutscher Peter* and not by the *Eisen-Lotse*, because today he'll sell more in front of the *Deutscher Peter* than in front of the *Eisen-Lotse*.

Can I have an ice cream? I ask Mother.

No, Mother says to me.

And me? my sister asks.

You can't either.

Meanwhile Father, who was already with Herr Veilchenfeld very early in the morning and applied a head bandage and now, supported by his cane, is standing with us in the market place, is wondering: Where could Herr Veilchenfeld go? For the poor fellow is without connections, indeed no one will have him.

He can't go to anyone in the photo in his cabinet anyway, they're all dead, I say. They used to play together, but now they're dead. Can we really not have ice cream, I ask Mother.

No, Mother says to me.

Besides, Father says to Mother, he doesn't want to go away. As strange as it sounds, he's actually attached to the area. He has become used to it.

Meanwhile Dr Magirius, who has come to our town by train from Russdorf and has gone from the train station to the market in his braces, his jacket over his arm, and having examined both the *Deutscher Peter* and the police station, now steps over to us with head bowed. Suddenly he points with his outstretched right arm at the surrounding houses, at one after the other, and says that after what has happened our town can never be the same again.

Shh, says Father, not so loud.

Never the same again, he says. And after he learned of the matter early in the morning, by a shout up to his window, at which he had just been standing—after Father had already been by Herr Veilchenfeld too—he had brought a bouquet from his garden to the bedside, gladiolas, as if he were already dead. And really Herr Veilchenfeld looked that way, too, and had not made a sound. The first thing that Herr Magirius does is to look in the kitchen for a vase for the flowers, but he doesn't find any. Then he lays the flowers at the foot of the bed in which Herr Veilchenfeld is lying, and looks down at Herr Veilchenfeld, who is probably still lying there just as when Father left him, that is, covered up to his neck, his head bound, his arms on the cover.

Oh, Bernhard, Herr Magirius says, and bends over him.

And hopes, naturally, that Herr Veilchenfeld will now also say something and perhaps it will become a conversation, but Herr Veilchenfeld says nothing. Oh, Bernhard, Herr Magirius says again and pulls the window curtain back, so that Herr Veilchenfeld, even if he says nothing, will at least see a little better. Then he goes over to the other side of the bed in order to look at him from the other side and to talk with him from the wall. Oh, Bernhard, says Herr Magirius and waits a little, but then Herr Veilchenfeld just turns his bandaged head away, so that he doesn't see Herr Magirius any more. Then, because Herr Veilchenfeld says nothing and gives him no sign of life, Herr Magirius goes past the foot of the bed out of the room again and forgets the flowers, which have now surely wilted in the heat and which can now be thrown away.

And why don't we get any ice cream, I ask Father.

I can't tell you that, says Father, but I can tell you what you will get if you are not quiet immediately.

And when Herr Magirius asks Father how badly injured Herr Veilchenfeld is, Father thinks for a moment and says: He doesn't speak any more, my dear Magirius, that's what is worst.

What, Mother asks, he says nothing at all any more?

Nothing at all, says Father.

Now, says Herr Magirius and writes something on the

pavement with his walking stick, but I can't read it, and Father probably can't either. Then he points over at the *Deutscher Peter*, where the people are standing, and says: If they knew what kind of people there are here, they wouldn't be standing there so calmly.

What would they be doing instead? Father asks him.

I don't know what they would be doing, says Herr Magirius, but at any rate they would not be standing there so calmly.

Oh, my dear Magirius, they know indeed, Father says to Herr Magirius and gestures dismissively.

You think so?

But of course, says Father.

Then Father and Herr Magirius stand close together for a while in the morning sunshine and wonder whether the people know it and, in order not to fall, maybe even lean against each other, and I wonder who is leaning on whom, the hefty Herr Magirius on Father or the other way around, since both have something wrong with their legs and cannot tolerate so much strangeness. Anyway, Father and Herr Magirius regard the people in front of the *Deutscher Peter* and the police station for a long time and wonder if they know something, and if so, how much, and Herr Magirius says no, they know nothing, and Father says yes, they know everything. And the people look over at us and recognise us little by little and wave and call: Good morning, Doctor! and: Splendid weather today! And we don't know whom they mean, Father or Herr Magirius, and so both return their greetings and call out: Good morning! and Very true! because both are polite and both are doctors.

Then Father says, he thinks about Herr Veilchenfeld every spare minute and wonders if he should really go away and to where and if possible overseas for the couple of years that he still has before him.

His heart, Herr Magirius asks, is certainly not the strongest?

The strongest, says Father, it is not.

How many years does he have left then, approximately, asks Herr Magirius, but Father does not want to commit himself so exactly, because for him, as the old saying goes, everything is in God's hand.

The main thing is that he doesn't harm himself, says Mother, who has already heard of such cases.

And why may I not go to him any more, I ask, because I saw Herr Veilchenfeld on his "stroll" only from a distance and would gladly have once seen how he looks without hair. It would really be a completely new Herr Veilchenfeld, because he also doesn't talk any more. Would I still recognise him, I ask.

Yes, says Father, probably.

And me, asks my sister, would I too?

Yes, he says, you too.

And Herr Veilchenfeld, I ask, would he recognise me with his bandage?

Yes, says Father, he would.

But how can he recognise me if you have bandaged his head, I ask.

Because I have left him two holes for his eyes and one for his mouth, Father says to me.

And for his nose, I ask, have you left him any for his nose?

Yes, says Father, for his nose too. And now, he says to Herr Magirius, I will venture a shocking pronouncement for a doctor. But perhaps in light of what is coming for Veilchenfeld, it would not be the worst thing, if he were to kill himself, says Father, whose thinking in many things is tougher than Mother's, and who also says these thoughts aloud.

Well, says Herr Magirius, to suggest that to him would indeed be going rather far.

Yes, says Father, it would be going far.

We really should go, Mother says, we have seen everything.

Yes, says Father, we are going now.

After lunch we sit in the ground-floor room just as when Herr Veilchenfeld was with us, except that the table isn't pulled out now and Herr Veilchenfeld isn't here. Instead he is lying by himself on his sofa and trying to read, Father says to us. Mother has gotten the knitting things and sat down with us in order to finally finish knitting the yellow pullover for my sister. She says it's remarkable how much can be said about a single person like Herr Veilchenfeld in such a small town as ours, without his ears burning.

Don't your ears burn when someone talks about you? she asks me.

No, I say, they don't burn.

Well, people do indeed only talk about Herr Veilchenfeld when they are among themselves. As soon as a stranger approaches them, they immediately talk about something else and then merely think about him, because it doesn't leave any evidence. I think about Herr Veilchenfeld too sometimes, but I don't tell anyone. And I would gladly have seen him once again, but I must put the idea of a visit to him right out of my mind because it is too dangerous, says Father, who goes to him in his flat every second day, to look after his heart and his head. As soon as he steps into the corridor, he calls out loud that it is just him, so that Herr Veilchenfeld is not frightened. But sometimes he's frightened anyway. Then he turns completely pale on his sofa and pulls the woollen blanket to his chin and begins to hum, like the time at our house when he couldn't drink the coffee. Then Father always says the same thing at the door: Calm yourself, dear fellow.

I am somewhat nervous, Herr Veilchenfeld says, but otherwise I lack nothing.

I know that, says Father and walks into the cabinet and puts his bag on the chair by the sofa on which Herr Veilchenfeld has stretched out under his blanket and is already reading or turning pages again. Then he has to put the book aside and sit up and open his shirt and breathe deeply and cough, so that Father can hear his heart and his lungs clearly and can prescribe something for him, but which won't help him either, if he does not finally stop having so many thoughts about everything.

You should look a little more cheerfully at the world, Father then says to Herr Veilchenfeld.

And what should I do in order to look more cheerfully at the world, Herr Veilchenfeld asks Father, and buttons up his shirt again. But Father can't tell him that either, because he himself isn't cheerful and sometimes doesn't laugh for months, Mother says.

It is much easier to treat Herr Veilchenfeld's head because it is external, and therefore cheerfulness doesn't matter so much. The bandage is simply removed and new salve applied and a fresh bandage wrapped around, so that one no longer sees the wounds. Then Herr Veilchenfeld looks once more as if he had fallen from a tree or as if his head were mostly artificial, and not like yours or mine. When he's leaving—he has snapped shut his doctor's bag once more—Father says that he will shut the flat door once more from outside now, so that no one can get to him and that now he is attractive once more and can look for a bride. But this doesn't mean anything, because Father says that to all his patients, even if they are over eighty and must die soon. Only he doesn't thump him on the shoulder any more, because Herr Veilchenfeld didn't like that the first time already, but instead rather gently removed his hand, if Father remembers correctly. Because as a doctor, he is always out and about and sees and hears so much that he sometimes wonders if he has seen and treated a particular patient himself, or has just read or dreamt of his case, or simply invented him.

Now we haven't seen Herr Veilchenfeld for a long time, not even near his beanpoles, so I sit at the table in the big room downstairs and draw for him a couple of houses and a marketplace, all from our town. Those that he can't see at the moment, so he doesn't forget them. Then I roll up the drawings together and stick them in the letter box on his courtyard door, from which he must have picked them up, because in the morning they have disappeared. (Assuming someone else hasn't picked them up.) Sometimes when I walk by under his windows along Höhler's fence, I think I see Herr Veilchenfeld's head, wrapped up in a tremendous bandage. His mouth is of brown leather and sewn up tightly. But if I then stop and want to examine him, he has disappeared. Probably he feels ashamed in front of me. Or I have just imagined his face. At any rate, I now also say to myself: It would be best if he killed himself. And: Now he has killed himself! But then I see Herr Veilchenfeld again at the window, and he is still moving around. Well, then he will just kill himself tomorrow, I think and continue on. Yet when I come by his house the next time—I've made a detour on my way to school—it's light again, and Herr Veilchenfeld is sitting at the bay table and thinking and writing everything down. Not yet, he is still writing, I think and I go slowly past his house. But Herr Veilchenfeld is also still living on the following days, even if he isn't always writing, but perhaps playing piano instead, which means that he has written something or soon will be writing something, says Mother. And she takes my hand and leads me along Heidenstrasse, because she has to buy a hot-water bottle for herself at Herr Hafermeier's. And she recognises Herr Veilchenfeld playing and says: Now he's playing Brahms. Or she says that he's playing Mozart.

Yes, I say, I can hear it.

Or he plays a popular song from his youth that Mother has never heard either or has temporarily forgotten and I temporarily hear those unfamiliar sounds in my head, because I may not stop and look up and listen to him.

For Mother still has her colics, but they are no longer so severe. Instead they are such that she can bear without calling Father and without Father having to give her an injection right away. Father stays in the office and doesn't know where they come from either, maybe from the many worries. Mother often lies in bed upstairs and cries and has the blinds down, so that her face can't be seen. Then Aunt Ilse has to come here again and stand in the kitchen, and Father goes around the house smoking and waiting for the meal. At the table we talk about my sister, who should be going to school, but she doesn't want to.

I don't want to, she shouts again and again and stamps her feet.

But don't you want to grow up, Margarete, Aunt Ilse asks and serves the food.

No, I don't want to grow up either, my sister shouts, and then Aunt Ilse can only shake her head over so much unreasonableness and go into the kitchen again.

At this time everything is changing in the world, but especially in our town, and the older people can only sigh, because they have not reckoned on these changes, Mother says in her room.

What's changing then? we ask.

Everything, says Mother.

What we notice: Our town is becoming larger. If we were recently still only fifteen thousand, now we're nearly eighteen. Indeed there are also people moving away, but in exchange new ones come. Others disappear overnight, and when we ask Mother about them, she says, that's no concern of yours. They leave their houses wide open or leave the doors slightly open, and you can go into the flats and houses, where the tables are still set and the cushions are rumpled. There is even food still on the plates, but there are often flies sitting on it. You can look around and go through the room and, if you want, take something from a table or from a cupboard and throw it against the wall, which Herr Schmittchen's grandson does sometimes. He takes a cup, full or not, and maybe smells it and cradles the cup in his hands, then he throws it against the wall. Or against a cupboard or through a window, and then everyone laughs and shouts: Boom! and they clap their hands. Or you stick whatever appeals to you in your pocket and take it home with you, which, even if it's forbidden, others do, those who one would not have thought would do so, Father says to us and directly runs back again to Mother, because she's calling again. Also entire shops disappear, like Eplinius & Hirsch, which, having had no customers for months, is attacked one night. When we slowly go by it the next morning with Mother, the shop windows are smashed, and the pieces of broken glass are lying on the pavement; you can cut your shoes on them. So please don't walk on them, Mother says and leads us around the broken glass. In the shop, the fabrics are lying on the floor, and young Lansky, who usually stands in the train station behind the baggage counter, is stamping around on them in his railway boots. I will never forget his stamping around that way on the fabrics with his boots, Father says, and we don't need to greet Kalle Lansky and the others who've also been stamping on them any more. Now the shop stays closed for a long time, and only when new windows are put in and the displays are changed is it opened again and now it's named *Bauer's Fashion House*, while the Hirsch family are in Zurich and Herr Eplinius is in New York, where hopefully they are in a bad way, Herr Lohmann says. Also after Easter Bernhard Schloss doesn't come to school any more, and Herr Lohmann collects the books that he left lying under his bench during the long recess. For this purpose he puts on special gloves. To be pulped, he says and goes to Bernhard's seat and throws the books into a cleaning products carton and, with the door wide open, carries it out. In order *to jolt our backwater into action*, Father says, a Herr Gipser is sent to us. But this will be no picnic, he'll have a difficult time of this, he says, as Herr Gipser arrives.

Herr Gipser, when he grandly arrives, is driving ahead of a furniture van from the firm of Schenker, because this furniture van won't find the house without me, Herr Gipser says to himself. But because he doesn't know our town either, Herr Gipser loses his way again and again and the furniture van does too. We run the last part behind them, so we can watch the unloading, and lean against the opposite wall and see everything perfectly. Mother gets up this morning too, because Herr Gipser is coming, and gets dressed warm underneath, and goes past us in a hurry to look at Herr Gipser and his furniture, too. And she can't take her eyes off him at all, although now in fact she can see him every day in all his handsomeness when he walks through the streets in his high boots, to get himself used to us and to shout at the people that they should buy themselves a bigger flag, Father says to us. In any case Herr Gipser must steer his open convertible through our streets with one hand, because he lost the other in the struggle against *the rabble*, as he tells everyone right away. Even so, he manages to honk three to four times at every street corner. Frau Gipser, as she climbs out of the car, has round, fat shoulders and wears a hat shaped like a discus. She has disappeared into the house hurriedly and will seldom be seen in the coming years. When we've watched how the furniture goes into the house for a while, Herr Gipser comes over to us and offers us raspberry sweets from a sticky paper bag. And, when we've each taken one, says that each of us may take two and that now everything will be different and, in case we wanted to watch, we could lean on his fence, because we'll see everything better from there. And he goes back into his garden, where, from atop an empty beer crate, he shows the furniture movers with his one hand how best to take hold of and carry the individual pieces of furniture. Later Herr Gipser takes off his jacket and hangs it on the fence that we are allowed to lean on, only not where the jacket is hanging. His shirt is completely sweaty from shouting and has two breast pockets, from which two laces stick out, which connect the pockets with one of the shirt buttons. From the laces, which, as Father says, are also called *monkey swings*, there are whistles hanging, only you can't see them because they are stuck inside the pockets. But maybe he blows a whistle sometimes, I tell my sister, although he doesn't blow it on this day.

When we drive along Helenenstrasse on Saturday, it is the same crowd as before, I say to Father later. I am driving with him to Frohna, to pick up eggs from Herr Verhören, so that we don't have to eat the spinach, which Mother is washing, without something.

Only the crowd is now differently gotten together, Father says to me and drives slowly back home with the eggs. Here the streets are not yet paved, and many trees are still standing. The town is so cramped and overfilled that it will burst at the seams, he says. It will be built up everywhere, too. The remotest rural houses and farmsteads, which until now have been connected to our town in name only, are getting water and electricity, and the roads that lead to them are cobbled, if not asphalted.

Do you know what that is, Father asks me that Saturday, as we slowly drive by a freshly built, very ugly house.

No, I say.

Building madness, says Father.

Which has now seized our town, even if no one knows where it comes from so suddenly. Father doesn't either. Mother is still in her room a lot, although she isn't lying down so much. Instead she mostly sits in front of the mirror and looks at how she is becoming older. She suspects the building madness comes from the brick works that has been built south of us and that supplies our entire district with bricks and cement. It requires an entire day to go through the brick works, says Herr Lohmann, who with his wife, who probably has a glass eye, went through it once over one weekend and looked at everything. So you can just imagine how big the brick works is and how much work there is, he says. Go through it and you will see what work means, Herr Lohmann announces. While Father says that in our brick works no more work is done than in other brick works in the world. If anything, less, he says. And even if we wanted to, we couldn't go through it at all, because a high wall was built around it that allows no one to enter. At all events, the emerging building madness, in conjunction with the brick works, is overwhelming many of us. They are erecting and extending everywhere, even by us at the stone quarry. Almost overnight, in front of our parents' bedroom, blocks of flats were put up which make noise, dirt and shadow and our entire life, mark my words, will be ruined, says Father to Mother and to us, while in our ground-floor room he is agitated and limps back and forth. The good air that we always had will be breathed in and out, spoiled and consumed by the many people who are moving out to us now and in front of our windows, so that our air can hardly be distinguished any more from the polluted town air, Mother says to us. And she forgets her colic and gets upset, but everyone is getting upset about something during the time of the building madness, so that we completely forget about Herr Veilchenfeld.

He is ill, says Mother, when I once remember him and ask after him.

He lies on the sofa and reads, says Father.

If he isn't already relocated, says the young Frau Verhören, who is pregnant again, and crawls into her chicken coop to collect the eggs for us.

Where is he being relocated to, then, I call after her in the chicken coop, but Frau Verhören doesn't know either.

At any rate, he isn't sitting in his bay, at least not at the window. But it doesn't matter, because with the new conditions, it wouldn't be possible for Herr Veilchenfeld to get out of Father's automobile anyway, not without being seen in our courtyard, which is now flanked by blocks of flats, and be able to walk around it, in order to eat dinner with us. Anyone who goes in or out of our house is seen by the neighbours, who after moving in, got cushions and laid them in their windows and (because otherwise there's nothing else to see), look into our courtyard and monitor who goes out and in. But probably, even if he were not seen, Herr Veilchenfeld would not want to eat with us any more, so that in the year of building madness I can forget about him easily.

When Father came home, first we could see his old automobile through the open window and then hear his artificial leg clatter. He left the automobile parked outside and he came in on the leg. We heard how he hung his oaken cane on the hook. He came from Herr Veilchenfeld. He looked at Mother.

What is it again now, I'll scream soon, if I hear that name one more time, cried Mother, who always got a colic when she heard the name Veilchenfeld, and would have preferred not to think of him any more.

We sat down at the table. First Aunt Ilse brought the tea, then the bread and the sausages and the cheese. Frau Malz, who had followed Frau Bichler and had been cleaning two times a week at Herr Veilchenfeld's, now wasn't coming any more. Instead, this afternoon, when she didn't have to come at all, she appeared at Herr Veilchenfeld's accompanied by a sinister and moustachioed man, whom she called her "brother-in-law" and who carried a raffia bag. Without knocking, she walked with her "brother-in-law" into the cabinet of Herr Veilchenfeld, who had drawn the curtains and was sitting at the middle table, reading a book.

Yes? asked Herr Veilchenfeld, who was now speaking again, if somewhat more quietly than before. If you didn't pay careful attention, you no longer understood him. Yes, Frau Malz, he said.

Then Frau Malz and her "brother-in-law" who, to give her strength, had put his arm around her shoulder, said that she would not be coming any more.

But why? asked Herr Veilchenfeld, and he made a slight movement of alarm over the book he'd been reading.

No, said Frau Malz and shook her head.

Then she went into the kitchen with her "brother-in-law," quickly made strong coffee for him and for herself, and laid everything that belonged to her—her apron, her housecoat and her hideous hair net—in the bag, but also the dusting and wiping cloths that did not belong to her at all, but instead to Herr Veilchenfeld. And she disappeared with the "brother-in-law," who had come with her in case Herr Veilchenfeld should have offered any resistance or been violent, into the steady rain then brewing, Father told us. And he pointed at the window, outside of which the rain was still falling.

Father now regularly listened to Herr Veilchenfeld's heart and once described to us how not only Herr Veilchenfeld himself, but also his flat, was deteriorating. His own deterioration

began with the heart; that of the flat, with the kitchen. Once
a jar of honey, from which he sometimes took a spoonful,
had fallen on the floor, and he had stepped in it and, without
noticing the sticky mess on his feet, had walked through the
entire flat. Anywhere you stood now, if you then moved
around, honey stuck to you. Father had also once been in
the kitchen, but he no longer went in there.

And why not, I asked.

No, said Father, and shook his head.

Please, I said, describe it to us.

But Father did not want to describe Herr Veilchenfeld's
kitchen to us.

When Father came back to the cabinet from the kitchen,
where he had wanted to wash his hands, Herr Veilchenfeld,
who was still sitting on the sofa with unbuttoned shirt,
turned suddenly to Father. And, even though he was not
cheerful, he laughed out loud in Father's face.

Yes, what is it, Father asked him.

Isn't it, Herr Veilchenfeld said to Father.

Indeed, Herr Veilchenfeld's cabinet was also no longer
what it had once been, if Father had seen it accurately during
his visits. For as Herr Veilchenfeld could not clean the cabinet windows himself, the dirt and the dust lay ever thicker
on the panes, and ever less light came in. Twilight lay over
everything, even at midday. And Herr Veilchenfeld preferred
not to switch on the electric light, except for the reading
lamp, so that his shadow was no longer visible from the street.
So that they thought that he had moved away, that the flat
was already empty.

The books lying in the darkness are especially eerie, Father
told us at the table. And then it struck him that Herr Veilchenfeld, when something falls on the floor, absolutely no longer

stoops to pick it up. In protest against his situation, which is making his body become lethargic, Father says. He also may no longer enter the town park, where he looked at the water with such pleasure and where there are swans now, too. They were acquired in the course of the beautification of our town. The big ones are very smooth and white and bite right away, while the little ones are grey and fluffy and not yet swans, so that you always want to touch them, but you may not do that either. Herr Veilchenfeld also may not sit on the benches in front of the park any more. Herr Geier, with his uniform cap on, although otherwise in civilian clothes, brought the announcement of the prohibition to him in his flat to sign, so that he has been given notice of it and does not sit on a bench one day and then say that he did not know about it.

Does he leave everything lying that he's dropped, I ask and imagine a room in which everything that falls down remains where it fell.

Not everything, says Father, but a good deal.

We nod. Outside an aeroplane roars over the house, and Mother puts her hands over her ears, either because of the aeroplane noise or because she doesn't want to hear anything more about Herr Veilchenfeld.

At all events he needs a household helper, Father says, so that he doesn't go further downhill.

So Herr Veilchenfeld, who was still frightened and who still wasn't leaving his house, let Dr Magirius put up a note in the post office, on which he had written in his neat scholarly handwriting: Older, academically learned gentleman, *Professor emer.*, in exceptional circumstances, but very quiet, seeks a household helper over fifty, twice weekly, well paid. 26 Heidenstrasse, 1st Floor. His name was not on the note, but we knew at once anyway who had written it, and we wondered if he was allowed to simply hang a note up in the post office, and whether anyone would reply. Most of us thought no one would reply, because no one could imagine who would clear away the mess of *such a person*. Others thought, no, someone will reply, there are actually not so many jobs, but certainly more than two or three would not reply, but they too were mistaken. It turned out that we had overestimated the difficulty of finding a household helper for Herr Veilchenfeld. He was quite overrun. First came an old blonde spinster, but her hair was probably dyed. When she saw Herr Veilchenfeld's shorn head and the condition of his kitchen, she cried out Oh! and went away again. Some, when they read his name, already left at the front door. Those who just wanted to see the inside of his flat and did not want to work for him at all, followed him with rapid secret glances through all the rooms, ran their fingers through the dust, which lay on all the furniture, and disappeared again. Others went with him into the cabinet, sat on the examination seat and had the work explained and where in the flat everything was. Perhaps they would have taken the position too, but fearing they could become *involved* in something, they disappeared also. Others were afraid of Herr Veilchenfeld himself and considered him to be violent on account of his scars. A Frau Raabe, who was certainly over seventy and didn't get enough air any more and in her application obviously had thought only of the additional income and not of the work, was sent away by Herr Veilchenfeld himself, after he had pressed a two-mark piece in her hand. Finally, on the fourth day, a bony, coarse and loud person came, named Frau

Abfalter. At the sight of the rundown kitchen, she emitted a kind of battle cry, ran for the wash bucket and pounced on Herr Veilchenfeld's dirt as if it were completely normal. Instead of closing the room doors gently, she slammed them with all her bodily might, which naturally did no good for Herr Veilchenfeld's heart, Father said to us. Thankfully, Herr Veilchenfeld hardly saw the new help. When she entered his flat in the morning, he locked himself in his cabinet and retreated with a book to the outermost point in his bay. The whole time she was in the flat, he either looked at his book or at the street below. He was afraid of the noise that she made, and was disgusted by her, while Frau Abfalter had no feelings about Herr Veilchenfeld, as she told people in town. To clean, she put on rubber gloves that reached to her elbows, and when she had to knock on his door, she knocked with the broom handle. But Herr Veilchenfeld came out of his bay only very rarely; he called out whatever was necessary through the closed door. She called him—always through the door— first "Professor," then "Veilchen" and finally "Hey," and when he did open the cabinet door, planted herself in front of him, with her hands on her hips. Since she washed the corpses in the town cemetery, nothing horrified her any more. A clumsy boor, a textbook example, who will bleed him dry, says Father.

Then Mother became ill again, but it was definitely not her gall bladder. Instead, Father said it came to her from her head, she distressed herself so. Then we had to go into her room and heat the room, because the winter, which had come suddenly, was so hard that the frozen birds fell out of the trees like black fruit. Then we could see him for the first time at close quarters again. One time at midday, in a fleece coat, with gloves and scarf, in the winter sunshine near the *Lampenputzer*, but where it wasn't dangerous at that time of day. He had dwindled. If he were laid in a coffin, it could easily be in a child's coffin, Father said to us. We saw his hair now, too, because, as if he were proud of it, he had not put on his hat, so that anyone could see it, while we were wearing thick woollen hats with colourful pom-poms on them. Now, Herr Veilchenfeld's hair was really awful! With his hair he actually looked as if he could be almost violent, at any rate frightening. We stopped, and I winked at him. Then Herr Veilchenfeld stopped too, looked around in every direction, winked back and said: I am panting, you hear? Because I always walk somewhat faster than I can.

We said hello.

And because naturally, Herr Veilchenfeld said, I want to be back home as quickly as possible. Then he asked how we were.

Good, I said. And you?

Also good, obviously, he said and smiled.

Then he asked me how I was coming along with my drawing, whether I was now holding the pencil correctly.

Oh, I hold the pencil correctly now, I said, but I'm not much farther along yet.

The courage is lacking?

Probably. And you, are you still drawing? I asked, because nothing else occurred to me.

No, he said, I'm not drawing any more.

And why not?

But he didn't tell me that. Instead, looking around all the time, he leaned his back against the wall of a house and said, Let's hope no one sees us.

But there's absolutely no one here who could see us.

I hope you're right, he said. Has no one told you that you may not stop, when you see me on the street?

Oh, we've been told already.

And?

Oh, I said, it doesn't matter at all if we stop for a bit.

And you also may not speak with me, that is also forbidden, he said. It's better if you go on and forget whom you have seen, he said, and tried to shoo us away.

Who've we seen then? asked my sister.

But we haven't seen you at all, I said.

Then Herr Veilchenfeld laughed and winked again, but then he was serious right away, came still a little closer and whispered in my ear: There is nothing that I could draw, it's all not worth it. There's no need to hold onto the world as it is, there's no point in that. And he shook his shorn and, as I saw by his ears, obviously ice-cold head. Then he came still somewhat closer and said: I come from far away, even if it doesn't look that way, from a deep infernal abyss. I've already been on the way for millennia, but I will not be for much longer. Then I will enter into the memory of Nature. And then, because a woman on her bicycle was riding directly toward us from the distance, Herr Veilchenfeld hurriedly thanked me for *the little works* that I had pushed into his letter box once, said nothing about whether he had recognised our town from the house entrances and house fronts, also said nothing of coming again or seeing us again, and wished us and our parents well, which sounded final. And, because the pavements had not been cleared of ice and snow every- where, he walked with cautious old man steps—so that I won't fall once more and have everything smashed up again, he said to himself—while going off again in the direction of our Town Hall.

What he now needs of course, and indeed very urgently, are emigration documents, said Father, who on account of the typhus, which had appeared suddenly among us and of which someone had already died, was always tired now, because they weren't letting him sleep. In fact, Mother yawned a lot too, but she could at least lie down in the afternoons, not to sleep, but rather to brood for half an hour, she said. The Hirschs had now gone away too, soon we were completely on our own. What a fine life it is becoming, Father said to us. Only Herr Veilchenfeld had forgotten to go away, although he too was now resolved to do so. Then I went to him for a second time and brought him a prescription from Father, but whether it would help, Father didn't know either. Suitcases were standing in the corridor; some were even standing in the cabinet.

Step over them, lad, just step over them, called Herr Veilchenfeld, who was standing in front of the bookshelves and wanted to pack up books. He just didn't know which ones.

I'm bringing you a prescription. Here, I said and held it out to him.

Very good, just put it down, said Herr Veilchenfeld, as if he didn't need the good medicine at all, and pointed to the overfilled middle table, on which there were already other papers lying under batches of books.

What does one take along, and what does one leave at home, asked Herr Veilchenfeld, and pulled ever more books off the shelves.

Surely you can't take all of them with you? I asked.

No, I can't carry them all.

Then just take the ones you need with you.

But lad, said Herr Veilchenfeld, I actually need them all. In fact, he had underlined something in all the books, whatever he needed for his new work, which he was probably writing non-stop, so that nothing would be lost. What should I do then, he asked me, but naturally I didn't know either. We stood there side by side in front of the shelves for a long time and considered what Herr Veilchenfeld could do so that what was marked would not be lost, but nothing occurred to us.

Take this with you, at least, I said and pointed to the photograph of the quartet, so that abroad he would also see how he had once looked and who his friends had been, but he shook his head.

I would certainly like to take it, he said, but I will forget it.

Then put it in a suitcase, then you won't forget it.

No, said Herr Veilchenfeld, I can't put it in a suitcase.

And why can't you put it in a suitcase?

Because I am not yet certain if I am really going.

So you're staying?

No, Herr Veilchenfeld called out very loud, just away from here.

And he looked from his bookcase—and I looked too— through the bay window, on which big raindrops were beating, at our town, which on such rainy days is naturally very sad. Indeed for him our town was sad without rain, too, and a trap, said Herr Veilchenfeld.

And why is it a trap for him, I asked Mother, who was just going to iron.

Oh, it has happened little by little, as many things simply happen little by little, Mother said and told us everything about Herr Veilchenfeld, as far as it was known to her. He was not going to write his last book in our midst, but in

Switzerland, where apparently he has found, after a long search in musician circles, a great-niece who will look after him. Yes, he will not stay much longer now, Father called out to us, as if he had just learned this through his wide-open surgery door, and he showed through the intonation of his words that he thought this for the best. Naturally it would be a loss for our town, to lose a philosopher brought here by chance, but few would notice the loss, so that one had to wonder if it was a loss at all. Anyway, for Herr Veilchenfeld, to be suddenly living in Switzerland would be a benefit. For while a philosopher both withdraws from the world and has to sit a lot with his writing, he must still have the freedom to go to the postbox whenever he wants, without having his head mangled straight away, Mother says at the ironing board. Meanwhile Father stands at the medicine cupboard and counts the boxes of medicine and wonders how he can explain to himself my interest in the small person of Herr Veilchenfeld, who can still make large difficulties for us. He cannot explain it, actually. Because really nothing ancestral or relational, no common interests or habits or background or age, nothing connects me with him, nothing. And although Father himself indeed once invited him to dinner, he calls my interest in him *pathological*, without knowing the pathology, and he continues to search for it. And, still in his surgery, still at the cupboard, Father comes to the conclusion, he calls out, that yes, Herr Veilchenfeld is so interesting to me because everything taught to me about the world and humanity, the entire remainder of Christendom, is shamed by the person of Herr Veilchenfeld. There we have a single case that belies all that we have taught the boy, Father calls out to Mother from his surgery, who is still ironing or already ironing again, but we too—we're sitting under the window—can hear Father. Such contradictions must indeed interest the boy, with his intelligence, he exclaims. And after a pause, because he is still not satisfied with his explanation: Last night, when I couldn't sleep, his reasons were clearer to me, but then I finally fell asleep, and now I can no longer think of them.

Sometimes, usually at night, a certain thought comes to a person, first as an obsession, then as a conviction, that doesn't let him sleep, Father says to us. The thought is hardly in his head when sleep is no longer possible. But at least for a couple of weeks it works for the person to push aside the thought, that will now always be there in the background, or at least not let the thought come near while falling sleep, and thus create a balance between thought and sleep. But in time, the thought becomes stronger and grows in meaning, consequence and significance, until it fills the room completely, including the bed. Of course then the thought is also lying within the breast of he who has it. Then the bed gets moved around from one corner to another in the hope that in this way you'll escape it, but the thought is everywhere. Meanwhile the strength to resist the thought diminishes and becomes weaker and finally hangs from the ceiling as a thin thread, and sleep hangs on the thread. So that the person then sleeps less and less and becomes convinced that he will never be able to sleep again, says Father to Mother and to me.

Later, when we are all sitting at the dinner table—Mother is also sitting with us—it turns out that it is not at all so easy for Herr Veilchenfeld to leave our town. The authorities are making difficulties, Mother says and brings the roast beef, though she may not eat any—at most taste a little piece. (But then she tastes two.) Almost every day one sees him, pale as a criminal, with hurried and determined but ever smaller little steps, moving through our side streets. To the Town Hall, Herr Veilchenfeld, but quickly! For he should have done this years ago: to try to get together his emigration papers. They're not making it easy for him now, says Father, who because of the typhus also has to go to the Town Hall, only to a different wing. He has to go to the *Health Wing*, while Herr Veilchenfeld must go to the *Travel Wing*.

But at the time, when he first came, he had not wanted to go away at all, I said to Father.

Based on mistaken assumptions, Father says and, like us too, he hasn't much appetite for the roast beef. So that we all sit there and smell our plates and, instead of eating, remind each other how after his arrival, on the basis of mistaken assumptions, he walked through our town for days, greeting everyone on all sides, in order to *settle in* amongst us. How idyllic, if sooty, our area was! How splendidly situated! How here he will finally be left in peace and allowed to breathe freely! Soon he knew all the houses and when they had been built or had collapsed. A methodical head, said Father, who knew Herr Veilchenfeld at that time only from a distance, but considered him *the methodical one*. If he continues in this manner, he will soon be better informed about us than we ourselves, Father had said. It was a mistake for him to come, Father later said. He should have climbed into the next train after his arrival, he says now, and gone away again, because now they won't let him any more.

This winter Herr Veilchenfeld has a notebook, in which he records every visit to our Town Hall in long, all-inclusive sentences, which then become ever shorter and finally are comprised of only single words. So that one day, when all this has been blown away from the face of the earth like an evil nightmare, he will still remember everything, says Father to us. He once walked over to the window at Herr Veilchenfeld's, with the notebook in his hand, in order to browse through it. A little black book with gold trim and thin black lines and some space after each day that had been completely filled with phrases like: Violet clouds, but also remarkable beneath. Our Town Hall from within. As supplicant over creaking floorboards to Room 6. Dizziness at entering, must lean against the wall, which thank God is just behind me. Or: Again at the Town Hall, this time in the room opposite. Wait for a long time beside one ancient Frau Estreicher, who, when I tell her who I am, strokes my hand. Had already heard of me, has the same fate. Because of the *fuss* that she makes, she is sent home. Or: Passport office, a clerical worker leads me inside. The clerical worker: What is your name? I tell it to him. The clerical worker: Yes, well, maybe you will receive a passport, one never knows. A staff member: Herr Thiele decides that, there is no need to discuss it. Yet another: No, Herr Thiele does not decide that, he only communicates the decision. One morning it arrives for him in the post; Herr Thiele then passes it on. At the entry to Herr Thiele's room, accordingly: A new delivery, Herr Thiele, one Veilchenfeld. But Herr Thiele is not there, nor in the adjoining room. When I want to go out again, I may not, I must step into a corner. I, joking: Am I arrested, but no one can tell me that. Dizziness again, sweating. Suddenly from the adjoining room the question, where are my documents. My documents? Where are my documents? In any case many of the documents that he needs for his emigration are not to be found, they must have been mislaid in the office or lost between offices, says Father, whose documents have not been lost and who can travel abroad at any time. And now in return for high fees collected from Herr Veilchenfeld the documents must be sought out, but none will be found, Father says. And when he wants to ask Herr Thiele about the documents, he must, so that he can even be admitted to his presence, pay a large sum to a charitable fund, although there is absolutely no connection between the charitable fund and his documents, says Father, as Mother steps toward us, one time, in front of the house. Sometimes they leave him standing in the corridor for two hours without taking any notice of him. He doesn't know whether they have seen him, whether he is even *permitted* to wait. Or when he is finally at the counter, they hang the sign "Closed" in front of his nose. Then in the notebook there is: The counter. The sign. The eyes behind the sign. My humiliation. My lowliness. Which of course doesn't help your heart, but indeed I don't need to tell you that, Father says to Herr Veilchenfeld, when he is examining him again one day. Yes, you are right, if I still want to go away, I will really have to get up earlier, Herr Veilchenfeld says to Father, when by chance—both have slowly descended from their wings—they bump into one another in front of the Town Hall and go home together. Though not through Helenenstrasse, which now is called something else, although we also still say *Helenenstrasse*, but instead through the narrow back streets, which our town also has, even if people don't use them, apart from Herr Veilchenfeld and Father and Mother and us.

Then he put on a fresh white shirt and his dark holiday suit with two buttons and one stay button, affixed a starched collar, which was not sewn onto the shirt, but was instead fastened on, and a tie, and he had to leave his flat before eight with a collapsible stool or emergency seat under his arm, which he would have been better off leaving at home, recounted Father, who, because it's nice weather, has seated himself in front of the house between the jelly and the coffee and, because his phantom foot is hurting again, has stretched out his false leg. And these flies, these flies! Although it is raining lightly, Herr Veilchenfeld goes without a hat, a little bent because of the wind, up to Hellmann the barber's, where the rainwater divides. The left stream flows downhill, the right disappears in the drain. Here he leaves the asphalted street and walks with his stool over *Reichmann's Field* along the backs of the houses. He also takes the roundabout way through Wikingergasse, just to avoid people. But that doesn't help at all, he's seen anyway. Frau Hudalik, who recently moved from Bohemia, sees him; Herr Maurer, who is shaving right by the window, sees him; the Limberg brothers, who because of their automobile, which is parked below, always have to keep an eye on the street anyway, see him; everyone in this poor neighbourhood, where everyone is coughing and there is still consumption, sees him, Father tells us, while he drinks his coffee. Herr Maurer even sticks his head out the window and calls out: Hey, where did you get that?

Do you mean me? asks Herr Veilchenfeld and he stops for a moment.

Yes, you, Herr Maurer calls out. That wasn't something lying around here?

No, it belongs to me, Herr Veilchenfeld says and raises his folding seat high up.

Well, if it's yours, then keep going, Herr Maurer says and waves him past his house.

If he had gone the usual way through Helenenstrasse, Father says, he would have attracted less attention with his stool. Because now, naturally, they wondered what he was up to with a stool in that rough district of our town at that hour. And then, my God, his walk! He must have developed it in his rear garden, since he has no space to exercise there, and instead always just crawls around the beanpoles. That has so spoiled the way he walks, Mother once said about Herr Veilchenfeld's walk. From pure fear of arousing displeasure—he never knows exactly how far he may go—there has been for some time something somewhat skulking and furtive and, when he has no hat on, *criminal*, about his walk, that *must* make people distrustful, she says. And everyone wonders what someone with such a walk is doing around here. It's his unhealthy life—the many sleepless nights, the crooked back, the pale skin because he gets no sun, as well as weak eyes, lungs, heart and so forth—that in the course of an unnatural scholarly existence a person is bent under, Father once said, for thankfully his profession takes him into the fresh air and amongst people. Naturally, because of the way he walks, Herr Veilchenfeld also attracts the attention of the people waiting in front of the Town Hall. What does a man, with desperation in his head and a folding seat under his arm, say when, in front of the Town Hall so early in the morning, he bumps into people, amongst whom of course there can also be the thugs from the summer? Does he say: Nice weather? Does he wish them good day? Herr Veilchenfeld, at least, doesn't say anything at all. Nor does he mingle with them, but instead positions

himself silently at a safe distance of three or four metres
along the Town Hall wall, against which he then also leans,
because I have advised him against this standing for hours
without holding on to anything, Father tells Mother and
us. When the Town Hall door opens, he lets everyone go
before him and goes in last, climbs to the *Travel Documents*
wing and stands in front of the passport office door at the
back. And, because now come the hours of waiting, he opens
his stool and sits on it, while the others, none of whom has
brought along a stool, have to stand. And they look down
at him disapprovingly, but at first they say nothing. After
all, he is probably the oldest of them, he's also frail, his knees
were already trembling while he was climbing, and after
climbing he was sweating too. But then in the passport office
room someone must have complained about him, for then
Seifert, the public official, suddenly walks out, plants himself
in front of him—yes, that's what they say now—says Father,
and asks him what this is all about. (Why he must sit, when
everyone else is standing.) Herr Veilchenfeld is so alarmed
by the tone of the question that at first he does not understand it at all. Then Herr Seifert says, has he indeed not
noticed then that he is sitting in the way here and hindering
the entire movement of Citizen Enquiries? And as Herr
Veilchenfeld moves over to the wall with the stool, Herr
Seifert waves him away and calls out: No, not there either,
there you'll just scratch the wall. And he simply takes away
the folding seat and carries it into his room, where Herr
Veilchenfeld may pick it up again when he goes home. So
that, after he has stood uselessly the entire morning and
waited for news about his documents, he must request his
stool upon leaving and must carry it across *Reichmann's Field*

again on the way home. Father tells us Herr Veilchenfeld is sorry that he also can no longer let me come to him for drawing.

Now Herr Veilchenfeld doesn't trust Father either any more because he thinks he lies to him sometimes. For example, he doesn't believe that he can live longer than three months with *this* heart, as he says quite openly to Father during one of his visits. Seated upright on the sofa, with his old man's chest exposed, the cold ear of the stethoscope over his heart, he looks Father in the eye and wants to bet him, that he has no longer than...

Let's do without the betting, says Father.

No, no, says Herr Veilchenfeld, really.

Oh, says Father, such wagers are offered to me again and again, even with money. Mostly out of cynicism, but often also out of great despair. Or from a desire for the truth, which they expect from me, but which I don't possess either. I'm not God, I lack that insight. Such wagers...

Four, says Herr Veilchenfeld, that I have no longer than four...

But Father raises his hand gravely and says: Hush, Veilchenfeld, do not sin against yourself.

In any case, Herr Veilchenfeld says, each of us will be sorry, when the other is no more.

Shush, Father says again, about non-existence there is nothing more to be said. And this silences Herr Veilchenfeld. But I know why Herr Veilchenfeld thinks this way and wants to bet him. To have to live and think in a once beloved landscape gently traversed by hills and comprised of forests (mixed woodland), which from inside outwards has grown repugnant and unliveable little by little, first sickens, then kills, Father says.

Sometimes, probably in a dream, I go to Herr Veilchenfeld for a drawing lesson after all and before I climb up, quickly call to ask him whether he wants me to visit.

Herr Veilchenfeld, I call, it's me, Hans, do you want me to visit?

And, pencils in hand, I am also dressed for drawing, wearing, for example, an artist's cap, as I once saw in the book *Drawing Pleasure for Beginners*. (I had no idea that I had such a cap.) And I ask, before I climb up, still hurriedly, how he is, but either he doesn't want to tell me or doesn't know himself. Then, to start a conversation, I just ask the time of day, but then he shakes his head. And his face is also much too thickly bandaged for a conversation. And he hasn't wound the clock, which is standing near the bay window on the bookcase, and amidst its ticking—it is just about to end—I sleep on, into the next dream. And dream that I'm going by Herr Veilchenfeld's house with Mother, and Mother says to me: Wave! And I wave to Herr Veilchenfeld, who's above, but he doesn't wave back.

But he doesn't wave back, I say, there, he doesn't make any sign.

Oh, well, he can't, says Mother and grasps me by the shoulder and tries to pull me quickly past his house.

And why can't he, I ask and I don't want to let myself be pulled, but instead stand still and look up.

Now, why would he not be able to wave, says Mother.

Because last night the neighbours removed his writing arm. And now come along finally, she says.

But how can they remove his writing arm, I say, horrified.

Oh, how already, Mother says, chopped off, chopped off of course. And as I break out in a sweat at the words *chopped off* and in no time have actually sweated through my new green-striped pyjamas, rear and front, I dream: Wait, this is a dream! But it can't be one, because I would have had to be asleep, but I am not sleeping at all. Instead I'm walking up Heidenstrasse in the sunshine with Mother, who is wearing her thin summer dress, which, because of the corset, really embarrasses me, until at the corner of Kreuzstrasse I become invisible with her and wake up from my dream.

When he comes down in the morning, he sees—smells—that someone has pissed into his daily milk bottle. He takes the bottle and carries it into the garden and empties it under the apple tree and carries it back to the house and puts it back where it was.

Then Mother says that his house was broken into, but it is worse. Oh, if they had just broken in and nothing else, she says. And she lies down again and has a colic again, although we wanted to stop for a bite to eat (at the *Linde*), and we stand in front of the house and hope that Father comes and that we will go to the *Linde* after all. And when we have stood there for a while, Father does come. And hearing what has happened to Mother, he quickly picks up a syringe and bounds upstairs to her, as quickly as he can bound with his one leg. And when he has given her the injection and the pain lets up, Father slowly comes back down and lets himself sink into his reclining chair and when we want to tell him, he knows everything already himself. And he says: Oh, children, it is terrible, because he had thought that everything was taken care of and Herr Veilchenfeld could finally leave, as he saw him going home with his stool.

Then he can't go? I ask.

Probably not, Father says.

So not everything is finished yet either?

No, says Father, it's just beginning. Because those at the Town Hall consider the business with the stool as a challenge and as insolence directed against them, Father says and wants to tell us everything, but Mother already feels better again and gets up again and comes down again and buttons her robe, so that we don't see her salmon-coloured nightgown. And as Father has promised not to talk *about him* any more today, we are going to the *Linde* after all. Mother just quickly puts make-up on her face and her lips and slips quickly into new stockings, so that she'll be warm below, while Father cleans the many dead flies off the headlamps of the automobile. Then we drive out to the *Linde*, because the table is reserved and it's Ascension Day only once every year. And because of the warm weather and the many people who all greet us and wish Mother a speedy recovery, this day we don't think of him any more.

After Ascension, in the *Rüdesheimer*, after the soup and before the roasted kidneys, Father took a letter from the Public Health Department out of his jacket pocket and pushed it over toward Mother. The letter informs Father:

"the patient Veilchenfeld, owing to diseases presumed to be hereditary, is no longer to receive medical treatment."

So: On Tuesday around eleven (in the evening) two open automobiles, in which a few young men were sitting, drove all around our town for a while, slowly and with dimmed headlamps. Some were also on the running board, some were singing, some not. They were seen here once, seen there once. It was as if they were looking for something for a long time that they were not finding. Others, who no longer fit in the automobiles and went on foot, find it faster. From the *Deutscher Peter* they cross the market and go up a bit of Helenenstrasse, then up Heidenstrasse, then they were there. And they begin to *take over* the bit of street in front of his house. Then the automobiles come too and are parked under the maple trees. The young people get out and call up to him: Hey, where'd you stick yourself, Violet? Or: Hey, you Violet, let us see you, don't always hide yourself in this way! Or simply: Hey, Grandpa, company! But Herr Veilchenfeld doesn't come to the window, simply hopes they will go away again, but instead there are more and more. Singing, they stomp up and down, shining their torches upwards through the branches of the trees, looking into the garden and finally, because they have run around enough today, sitting down on the kerb, from where they can see his window quite well. Then they take out their sheath knives and drag them over the kerb, so that there are sparks. So that Herr Blei, who was at the front during the war and supposedly stabbed a Russian to death with his bayonet, and who because of his moustache looks like Hindenburg and is called that, too, can't sleep because of the noise. First he walks over to his upstairs window, then he climbs down. He walks out his house door in his dressing gown, goes over to the youths, stands in front of them and asks what they want here.

We want to see Violet, but he won't let us in, he doesn't even come to the window, they say and point to the house.

What do you intend to do with him, asks Hindenburg.

We want to talk with him.

About what?

About everything, they say.

And what else?

Nothing else.

Is that really true? Hindenburg asks severely.

Yes, it's true, they say. And point up at the window and ask whether he's seen the light on in his place today.

No, says Hindenburg.

Oh God, they complain, and we have travelled so far, and now it's all for nothing.

And when Hindenburg once again asks, What do you want with him then? they say: Nothing, we don't want anything. What should we do then, if he's not there?

But Hindenburg doesn't know either. But then, as he sees their disappointed faces, he feels sorry for them, and he thinks for a moment and says: You know boys, you're worrying too much. When it's dark at his place, that doesn't mean that he's not there. He's usually there, always in fact. If I were you, I wouldn't whine this way, just try a little longer, then at some point he'll come. And having said this, he stops himself, with his fist in front of his mouth, because it's suddenly clear to him that he should not have said this, because now they won't go away any more. I should have warned old Veilchenfeld about them instead, he thinks. But then he says to himself, that Herr Veilchenfeld has surely heard them long before this, probably already expected their visit and did not need a warning and also therefore doesn't come to the window, because he knows they're standing around below. And other than not going to the window there's nothing more he can do. Surely he's locked the door to the building. Indeed it's weak and old; if a young man leans on it, it will fall apart. (And the door to his flat is the same.) So although Herr Veilchenfeld seems to live in a well-furnished, if also rapidly decaying cabinet, with carpet and books and a piano, he is in reality completely unprotected. It's as if he didn't live in a house at all, but in the middle of the street instead, where anyone can trample on him, Father says to Mother and to us. In any case, it is now too late to take Hindenburg's proposition—If I were you, I would just try a little longer!—back out of the air.

So he knows that you're coming? he asks them once again.

But he's waiting for us, they say.

So you have told him that you want to speak with him?

That wasn't necessary, they say, he knows it anyway.

And what will he say about the knives, asks Hindenburg and points at their sheath knives.

The knives, they say, have nothing to do with him.

Then you don't want to frighten him?

There's no reason to do that.

And what do you want to speak to him about?

Oh, they say, but he knows that, or he can work it out. There's no point in talking about it before we're upstairs.

Well, if he knows it, then it's okay, says Hindenburg, who lives in Number 30 and would not like to have anything scandalous happen in front of his house. Earlier he was patching bicycle inner tubes and now is sewing flags with his wife; he feels much more comfortable with that. Just don't do anything stupid, he says and goes back to his building's front door and shuts the front door behind him and climbs back upstairs.

Later making sparks became too boring for them, Father told Mother, so they begin to throw stones at his window, so that he'd finally show himself. But he doesn't show himself for a long time, he doesn't even hear the stones. In his fear, he ran into the storage space next to the bathroom, closed the door behind himself, climbed into an empty book crate and covered himself with the cover. And he thinks: So that I'm out of the world, in case they look for me, but at first they don't look. Until they lose patience and throw a few larger stones through his bay window and come through the garden to him in the building, smashing in the front door in the process, and that he hears. Then he climbs back out of the book crate, because hiding is pointless and they will find him anyway, smooths his trousers and jacket and his hair, which has grown back, takes a deep breath and opens the flat door, so that they don't smash that in, too. The visitors, larger than he, stand angrily before him.

Good evening, he says, what do you want?

But they don't want to tell him that, they simply push him out of the way.

Where are they, they ask, without looking at him, which room are they in?

Gentlemen, says Herr Veilchenfeld. Young men, he says.

You, Violet, which room are they in, they demand, and stand in the dim light of the corridor and surround and tower over him. From all sides, but always from above, their breath blows on him. Herr Urmüller, one of the patients whom Father can't help either and who looked them over just before the "storm," calls them: Big Children. And because they forgot to send them to school or to work and keep an eye on them, they were now standing there, he says. Or they sat on the kerb like hungry birds and spat. Herr Urmüller was naturally alarmed by these thoughts: Children, because children, as he knows, are capable of anything. They didn't even have the beginnings of beards yet, he said to Father. And in order to recognise their faces, he had bent far over them, but the last hint of daylight had disappeared behind the houses, and he did not see much. What he could hear well were their clear voices, with which they called out single words to each other through the darkness. Though even then it wasn't them he heard, but rather their collective convictions, their age or the surroundings they were born into, those in which they grew up. It all added up to threats of what was now about to come. The labourer Neumann, with diseased kidneys, 43, who's coming home tired from the brick works and shouts: Let me through, you! and pushes them to the side, tells Father that among their words had also been the word *corpse*. But Neumann is too *dead tired* to follow up on the word. For him a hard day is coming to an end, so he no longer hears so exactly. Only when he was getting up the next morning did the word occur to him again; then it frightened him, of course. Or it should indeed have frightened him, but perhaps he had misheard. Anyway, the kids all came from our town and spoke so like the rest of us, that's how Herr Neumann recognises them. Don't do that, you! he called to them in passing, but they didn't listen to him. Go home, old man! they had called out and waved him on.

And now they're standing around him in the corridor, but no one takes hold of him. Their fists are hanging at their sides or hidden behind their backs and they make sure that there is still a layer of air between them and Herr Veilchenfeld. Out of disgust at touching him or timidity or because they say to themselves, he's already as good as dead anyway. And they are still afraid of the dead, there is still that; as experience teaches us, it is a matter of habit, says Father and, when he tells Mother the story tonight, he lets his hands hang down from his chair, right and left, like two exhausted animals.

They also would not have looked him in the eye, but instead look past him, as the butcher, before he stabs an animal, doesn't look him in the eye either, he says. In any case, in the narrow seam of air that they leave him, Herr Veilchenfeld can still draw a breath and say something.

Young men, he says, what do you want from me. It is the middle of the night. You are in an unfamiliar house. There is nothing here that could interest you.

Then they exclaim: The books, Violet, where are the books?

And as Herr Veilchenfeld, oddly enough, does not immediately understand the word *books*, because he does not expect it from them—one understands only what one expects, says Father—or he does not want to tell them where his books are, or he has no air or no words for the answer, they lay their hands on his shoulders and push him aside and fling themselves—their young eyes see much better in the dark than his old ones—at the individual doors in his flat, tearing the doors open. The one to the kitchen, which at first they don't enter at all, the one to the bedroom with the doll's bed, the one to the storage space with the book crates, the one to the narrow bath.

Then one calls out: The books are here.

He is lucky, he is at the right door, before him lies the cabinet. And inside, up to the ceiling, the leprosy of the walls: printed matter. The others are at his side at once, penetrating into the cabinet. And now they let out their hate, which accumulated in them during their school days and later grew greater, on the books, says Father. And they tear the books from the shelves and shred them and stomp on them.

But gentlemen, he says. But as if he does not want to get in the way of their work, he does not go to them in the cabinet, but instead he backs away. And with his shoulder on the doorpost, supports himself, perhaps because he's nauseous too, and clutches the door handle tightly with white protruding knuckles. It was too much reality for him, says Father. And from the threshold he sees how they slowly go along the shelves and they rip the books that they don't like off the shelves, always three or four at a time, and through the bay window, which in the meantime had been pushed wide open—the hole in the pane was not large enough—they throw them into the front garden with the lilac bushes, which have already bloomed, or over the lilac bushes into Heidenstrasse, where they can be heard crashing down.

Young men, he says, gentlemen.

Don't get mixed up in something that's of no concern of yours, Violet, instead keep yourself out of it, you don't understand this at all, one of the children says and steps over to him. With manly, resolute steps, for he has boots on. And a cigarette between his fingers, so that there is smoke between them. So that the smell of Herr Veilchenfeld does not jump onto him. You understand that, don't you, asks the child.

Yes, says Herr Veilchenfeld and looks at the floor.

We have to...check everything, explains the child. The requirement is that everything...be checked.

I know, he said.

They belong to you, these...books, don't they, the child asks.

Yes, he says, they belong to me.

Have you read them?

Yes.

You see, says the child. Then his glance falls on the honey jar, out of which Herr Veilchenfeld, when he is hungry or tired, takes a spoonful. Without this honey he would have probably already collapsed, Father says to Mother and to us. The jar is standing at the edge of the middle table, he can barely reach it from the window.

What's that, asks the child.

Honey.

And what do you do with it?

I eat it, he says.

Eat, says the child and grabs the jar, totally unconcerned, totally cold. And opens the jar, stirs around with his finger and licks his finger. So you eat this, he asks again and puts the jar back.

Yes, says Herr Veilchenfeld.

Then the child takes a step back so that he can better look Herr Veilchenfeld over. Around his neck he is wearing a white scarf—it is merely rayon—like the Condor Legion pilots, whose faces he studies every day in the newspapers, which he takes with him at night when it rapidly grows dark in his parents' bedroom—he does not have one of his own. Like all the others, he has spent his entire life in our town and this night he has bumped into Herr Veilchenfeld unexpectedly. He marvels that such a thing exists. Herr Veilchenfeld doesn't fit in his handsome sleek head. The child has straight teeth and is slender and will also remain so, until he becomes coarser and more angular. His hair is curly blond, one long strand falls over his forehead. Inside a commonplace, but strong, skull a small number of beliefs that are simple, but robust, spread themselves. He has nothing against Herr Veilchenfeld, only he was told that he would be able to breathe more easily when he is out of the world.

Want one? asks the child and holds the cigarette packet out to him.

No, thanks, says Herr Veilchenfeld.

Then the child moves his hand a little, as if he wanted to stick it with his cigarette in Veilchenfeld's face. As if he's forgotten that Herr Veilchenfeld is actually dead already and that a corpse in a black jacket is leaning in front of him. Then he actually wants to kill him. The child is seventeen, perhaps eighteen, when he is standing beside Herr Veilchenfeld and wants to kill him. Someone has to do it, he says to himself. And he's worked up enough to kill, only no one would guess it. His breath is completely regular, his heart beats quite slowly. Hardly does an artery pulse in his temples, right and left. But then the child reconsiders and puts away the knife, which in his imagination he had already pulled out of its sheath. And merely tugs at the bashful, smiling Herr Veilchenfeld's ear, as he is now sometimes tugged.

An ear, he says.

Yes, says Herr Veilchenfeld.

Do you want us to cut it off for you?

No.

Don't you? says the child.

After they had thrown some part of his books—perhaps two hundred kilos—out the window and had trampled the newspapers and photographs that hung on the walls—the quartet, his dead quartet!—they went out again, Father told Mother and us. Through the corridor door, which is glazed but miraculously still whole. Where Herr Veilchenfeld had put up a note at eye level, with the opening times of the general store, which they also tore down and trampled on their way out.

Herr Veilchenfeld, in order not to attract attention, has gone into a corner.

So, Violet, they exclaim, that was it for today. And now nothing stupid, we're coming back. Now we know where you live.

As you wish, he says.

Then say goodbye to us.

Goodbye.

Well then, they say. And they tramp back down his steps and throw the books that had been flung out of the window into the automobiles and drift or drive home, tired but satisfied. So, this was at almost one, said Father. While Schindler, the former salesman and current postcard seller, maintains it was around midnight. Frau Stöck, who stood behind her curtain and did not let herself be seen and who saw them go into his flat and come out again, thought it had already gone two. But she was not tired, she could have watched for hours more. They also could not agree about the weather that night, said Father, who had conversations with six or seven patients who had observed the event. Herr Berger, our henpecked husband, thought it had rained; Herr Biele did not. Frau Miller-with-an-i thought it was a dark— Herr Schöpke said a bright—night with thousands of stars, which he even wanted to count, but then he didn't count them after all. For Frau Heuer it was certainly still June, although it had been Wednesday for a long time already, while Herr Müller-Saar, who shortly before his unpreventable death was able to speak briefly with Father about the matter, merely remembered a shooting star that fell on the jam factory. But what the weather was like, Herr Müller-Saar already could no longer say.

With the cigar—which as a good doctor he has forbidden himself—partly between his fingers, partly already in his mouth, Father tells us, after his morning visits and breakfast, of a drive to the flax-soaking pit, where the fifty-eight-year-old farmhand Lansky lies stretched out on his bed with his ulcerated leg, and tells Father, who cautiously presses on the leg, of his abhorrence of Herr Veilchenfeld, whom Lansky doesn't know at all. But he saw him from behind once and knew immediately what was happening there.

And what, asks Father and pulls the long silver needle deftly out of the bandage, do you dislike about him?

Lansky, without deliberation: The name.

Why?

It stinks.

Aha, says Father. And what else?

The nose.

And why that?

It's too big.

You of all people, Father thinks in view of Lansky's certainly not smaller, if also differently shaped nose, but says nothing. In any case, for Joseph Lansky, to see and to hate Veilchenfeld was the same thing. Because of his walk, too, he says, while Father, to spare him pain, does not unwrap the bandage, as he usually does, but instead cuts it off the leg with two sharp and clean cuts of his doctor's shears. Lansky has three big blond sons who live on bread soup and turnips, but when it comes to Veilchenfeld, thank God, they think like him, the old Lansky. Because today, too, despite Father's forbidding it, he got up again and was in the farmyard, he still has on his work shirt and his work trousers, both completely sweaty. The boots he had unlaced, but not taken off. For he was cutting wood during lunchtime, because doing that in the sun does no harm. And we have lots of sun this August '38.

But that is precisely what I have forbidden you to do, to be out in the sun, you jackass, says Father, who can't conceive of so much stupidity.

Oh, you forbid me too much, says Lansky, who doesn't trust Father because he thinks too much, and sometimes, when he's by himself, calls him a *thinking animal*.

Yes, forbidden, says Father. And he is so appalled at the condition of Lansky's wound, when the bandage is removed, that he can only murmur: Oh no, oh no! Then to bring Lansky to his senses, he even threatens him with the removal of his leg.

Then you will walk around like me, my dear man, then the wood will creak when you walk, he says and plays with his own, equally senselessly acquired, wooden leg that he brought back home from the war and that he now must unfasten and shove under his side of the bed every night.

But Lansky, whom in May he just cured of toxoplasmosis, which is actually an animal sickness, and in so doing possibly saved his life, doesn't listen at all. He wants to talk to him about Herr Veilchenfeld, with whom he seems to be completely obsessed. Just as if Herr Veilchenfeld, and not he, Lansky himself, were the patient threatened with mutilation and death. That such a wizened, bodily deficient person has so many giant sons! With his wasted leg, split at calf height by an axe while woodcutting and now ulcerating and swelling, stretched out far over the edge of the bed as if for the bone saw, his eyes shut tight, the sweat beading on his forehead, he suddenly calls Herr Veilchenfeld a *degenerate crippled beast* that should never have been allowed to enter our town.

Oh! says Father, why not then?

Because it was a mistake to let that beast in, Lansky says, and with blazing eyes looks around the gloomy shed, where he is at home. And Father is appalled and thinks for a moment, perhaps he still has the animal sickness. At all events Lansky is convinced that the nicest houses of our town, for example the Schrannen House, all belong to Herr Veilchenfeld, and that ever since he has been with us, he has secretly influenced everything happening here, and from his bay window is looking out all the way to him, Lansky, over the flax-soaking pit, directly into his window. And at that it is a good six kilometres from Herr Veilchenfeld to Lansky's room! Nevertheless, Lansky can always feel Herr Veilchenfeld's gaze. And when Father says to him that Herr Veilchenfeld is completely withdrawn from the town and lives without friends and, as far as he knows, has no income or assets beyond his pension, Lansky doesn't believe him and, because he can't fight back against the objection in any other way, begins to tread on Father with his feet.

Hey, Lansky, what are you doing, says Father, you'll make me all dirty.

Ow, says Lansky, ow.

So does it hurt you? asks Father, not really triumphing.

It hurts, Lansky moans, oh, it hurts.

And when Father says that since last year nobody in town speaks to Herr Veilchenfeld any more, Lansky says: I don't believe you! and even begins to foam at the mouth. Yes, Father thinks, it's as I thought, it will be the animal sickness again. And then, while he gently penetrates Lansky's wound with his tweezer and after a long search actually even finds a couple of bone fragments, Lansky declares to him that, if he should ever once see Herr Veilchenfeld walking alone through the woods or across the field, he would, with his own hands— he raises them high for examination—strangle him.

Lansky, says Father, control yourself.

Strangle, Lansky announces again and thrusts his wounded leg still deeper into the darkness of his shed. In his hate he seizes his other foot with both hands, as if to rip himself into two equal parts.

Lansky, Father shouts.

And his wild speech leads Lansky back to the probably unbearable pain in his leg. And Lansky will also have fever, for his wife, who has become quite tiny from giving birth to her three blond giants, is now bent low over him and has him ceaselessly drinking a dark and steaming concoction out of a bowl.

My good woman, leave that now, says Father to her, wishing to dislodge her from the bed.

No, he must drink because he's sweating so much, he will shrivel otherwise, the wife says, and what she pours into the sick man's mouth from above, immediately runs out through his pores further below.

Just away from here, thinks Father.

And, so that he can finally get out of the shed once again, into the fresh air, he quickly begins to apply ointment to Lansky's leg, and to bandage it anew, thus saving it for him a second time. But not without once again deciding to have a serious talk again with Lansky, who is certainly a victim of this lack of air. But hardly is the leg treated and bandaged again and Father is about to say Veilchenfeld's name for the last time, when Lansky rears up on his bed—perhaps he isn't aware himself—and curses Herr Veilchenfeld in every way, wishing him in a Hell which for the moment is not described in greater detail.

Quiet, Lansky, says Father, do not sin.

But Lansky curses Veilchenfeld.

Oh, you really can't be talked to, Father says and gives up. And packs swabs and tweezers and the bottle with iodine and the container of salve in his black doctor's bag, lets his brass lock close with a loud snap and is already standing at the shed door with his hat on his head. And there, while he bends down, in order to get out safely, Lansky straightens up in his place, supported by his little wife, and from his pillow forbids Father, who has told him in passing about Herr Veilchenfeld's heart condition, to treat him any more.

Well, then should I let him die? asks Father.

Yes, let him die, Lansky calls out.

But by then Father is already out the door. And thinks: Never, never will I let Veilchenfeld die, even if... And then forgets the end of his thought. And, appalled by so much hate, he goes hastily to his automobile with his creaking leg and away from there along the area's criminally neglected village roads.

Mother lies in bed for a long time, but then she is well again, and with her in the middle we go walking in the Hoher Hain. And we sit in the Amselgrund by the stream and don't get ourselves wet, but instead build a kind of mill out of branches and twigs and bark and then stick in wheels, because they are supposed to turn in the water, but the mill doesn't turn, and instead it floats away. Father and Mother sit on a bench with Pastor Lachmann as if they are on a stage above us and they look high up in the sky and then down at us. Mother, who sits in the middle, is wearing her floral dress, and doesn't have colic today, although no one knows when it will come next and whether the Amselgrund really does her any good. She is tired and needed three days to tidy up the kitchen again. How many hours the stove alone cost her! That's how Aunt Ilse thanked her for being allowed to help. Never, even if she lay dying, would Mother let her in her kitchen again, and certainly not near the stove. Really Father should forbid her to enter the house, but he hasn't done that yet, for if Mother becomes sick again, what will Father do? Now his walking stick is lying beside him, and his false leg is stretched out, so that his foot, which is no longer there, can recover somewhat. So Father and Mother, with Herr Lachmann, sit above us and look over our heads or look at us below. And they whisper and nod or are completely silent, so that we can't hear them, but we hear some anyway. Herr Wilhelm is so altered that Herr Lachmann can no longer recognise him, this is because of the bottle that Herr Wilhelm puts under his bed every night. Or Frau Miller-with-an-i, who will soon certainly get herself a divorce because her husband has someone else, even if he does not admit it. And poor Herr Lauger, who already can't see any more, now his hearing is also getting worse. Another couple of years and he won't hear anything any more, then he also won't come to hear the sermon any more, and in Herr Lachmann's church, which is never full anyway, there will then be one more empty place. While Herr Veilchenfeld...

Mummy, my sister calls, can we take off our shoes and go into the stream?

No.

And why not?

Because the water is too cold.

But here, where we are, the water is not too cold.

It is too cold everywhere, Mother says from the bench.

All right, so we don't go into the water, we walk along the water, which isn't so dirty here as it is farther on, after it's gone through our town. Once, we stick our hands in, in order to see how cold it *really* is. Anyway, Herr Veilchenfeld is now completely alone, because even Dr Magirius doesn't come to see him any more because of his legs, which are completely swollen and misshapen and would probably burst if he suddenly stood on them with all his weight and walked to Herr Veilchenfeld. And, as Herr Magirius says, *to crawl onto a cripple's cart and have oneself rolled to him*, no, he won't do that. He would rather write him a card now and then, on which is written: Hideous times, most esteemed associate, in which we are obliged to live. Or: But I am still reading, and you? And he moves the chair to the window when he reads because of the light, but there, too, he cannot see well enough, the windows of his house being too small for that. Or he falls asleep when he is reading. Sometimes he writes, too, about what he *has* read and how it has pleased him and of what it reminds him. Anyway, Veilchenfeld has been to the Town Hall now for the last time, Pastor Lachmann on his bench says to Mother and Father, and pauses.

Does he have the papers now? asks Father, as the pause comes to an end.

On the contrary, says Pastor Lachmann. And he recounts that last week Herr Veilchenfeld was at the Town Hall again, this time without the stool. So there he is, after he has been led into the passport room and more or less abandoned, after he was called into the inner sanctum next door, which is actually not open to the public. There he had to stand again. Then Herr Thiele entered, in his sharply cut suit on which one could almost cut one's finger, says Herr Lachmann, and he had Herr Veilchenfeld's passport in his hand and turned it back and forth, and Herr Veilchenfeld certainly believed that he would now receive the visa and be allowed to travel to Switzerland *after all*. Herr Thiele sat down and leafed through the passport once more and asked him a few more questions, such as his name, his address, and since when, and occupation or none; indeed everything corresponded with the entries in front of Herr Thiele.

So today you are how old, Herr Thiele asked and looked in the passport.

Today I am sixty-three years, eight months, two weeks and three days old, Herr Thiele, says Herr Veilchenfeld.

Then Herr Thiele in his sharp suit who, because he is always healthy and never counts his days and also cannot imagine that anyone could count them, smiled and called in two gentlemen, who were busy in the next room.

That's him, he said and pointed at Herr Veilchenfeld. According to his own declaration, he is sixty-three years, eight months, two weeks and five days old today.

And three days, Herr Veilchenfeld quietly amended.

Then the two gentlemen also smiled sympathetically and placed themselves to the right and left of Herr Thiele. Then

Herr Thiele became very official and laid Herr Veilchenfeld's passport before him on the desk and folded his hands over it and in a tone, as if he was going to recite something, said more or less: Professor Bernhard Israel Veilchenfeld, by virtue of the powers conferred upon me, I hereby revoke your German citizenship and expel you forever from our national community. And then, even before Herr Veilchenfeld could have nodded, Herr Thiele, in front of the two witnesses, tore the passport in two pieces, and then tore the pieces ever further, and, because it was too stiff to tear, he cut through the cover with a paper shears, which was easier. Until there was nothing left of the passport except shreds, which Herr Thiele piled up in a small heap in front of him. There, he said.

On the bench above us, Herr Lachmann told Father and Mother, Herr Veilchenfeld said: Herr Thiele, Herr Thiele, and shook his head, but Herr Thiele simply continued to tear and cut until the passport was beyond recognition. Then one of the gentlemen from the next room said: With your permission, Herr Thiele! and got a wastepaper basket and held it out to Herr Thiele, and Herr Thiele carefully thrust the passport shreds into the wastepaper basket. Then Herr Veilchenfeld quickly had to write out, date and sign yet another form in five copies indicating that he took note he was now no longer a German.

No? Herr Veilchenfeld asked.

No, Herr Thiele said.

And what am I now, Herr Thiele, Herr Veilchenfeld asked and put down the pen.

Certainly not a German any more, Herr Thiele said, and laid his flat hands down in front of him.

And what, Herr Thiele, does one do in such a case, when

after so many years one is suddenly no longer a German? Herr Veilchenfeld asked. Indeed I am nothing otherwise.

Now, what you do about that is your affair, Herr Thiele said, that you must decide for yourself.

And as Herr Veilchenfeld cannot immediately decide what is best for him to do, Herr Thiele says that in any case he cannot stand around in the Town Hall offices taking up his time, but instead must disappear, and indeed straight away. Go, go, cried Herr Thiele from behind his desk and he even hissed, in order to expel Herr Veilchenfeld from his office.

Then I am to go, asked Herr Veilchenfeld.

Yes, said Herr Thiele, to the door.

And as Herr Veilchenfeld at the door once more asks: And where does one go in such a case, Herr Thiele, when one is no longer a German, I mean in this town? Herr Thiele, who actually wanted to be in a good mood that day, shouts at him: Kindly don't ask such stupid questions, but disappear, or I will have you and your ridiculous bag forcibly removed from this building, which you have infested long enough.

But Herr Veilchenfeld preferred to leave on his own.

Not for nothing does our homeland have the shape of a heart, with our town right in the middle, says Herr Lohmann and runs the pointer over the map along the edges of our homeland. This is Russdorf, this is Frohna and this is Mittweida, which keeps growing larger too. While this here is our town, he says and points at it with his stick. A point without a circle, through which, look here, a line goes, the arterial and access road. And the face of our homeland, in which for centuries coal and ores have been dug, has scars and wrinkles. Such a scar is our town, and here too there was digging. Only nothing was ever found, unfortunately, otherwise it would look different here, says Herr Lohmann, with whom we now have not only German, but also Geography, and who because of idleness—the boy stinks of idleness—hauled me out of my window corner and sat me in the front, where he could monitor me better. In terms of commerce we are excellently well placed. And, if one discounts the fog in our air from the nearby brown coal industry, we ought to have a good climate too, only the sun cannot always get through the fog. We have exactly 18,562 inhabitants; we know that because we have just been counted, and our nearest major city is Chemnitz, which is nineteen kilometres away, yet the stench reaches us. But we are independent and do as we wish. In addition to the Hindenburg and the Pestalozzi schools—we attend the Hindenburg—we have a railway station, where the express trains do not stop, however, so that it can take some time, even if you are in a hurry to leave. Then a local court for minor criminals, a public swimming pool for swimmers and a slaughterhouse, at which many animals are slaughtered. The steeple of the Lutheran church is illuminated at night. From this steeple, as we all remember, a roofer fell to his death two years ago; no one at all speaks of this any more, just us! We discuss with Herr Lohmann, whose teaching is always lively, the question: What does a roofer do if he has climbed up on the church steeple with his son, who on his advice has likewise become a roofer, and the son takes a wrong step and slips, and can just hold onto his father's leg, and the father is holding onto the roof ridge. Answer: The father must shake the son off his legs, and give him a push, because he must figure that otherwise he himself cannot hold on much longer either and because it is better indeed if one falls than both fall at once. (Beside this son, the father actually has other children and a wife whom he must feed.) Because our town has no river, but only the stream that goes into our factories and comes out the other side again as sewage and stinks up the whole area, we may not go to Grüna any more, because we would have to cross the stream. And that is forbidden, Father says and drums his fingers on the table. It is also forbidden to go to Russdorf; that's where all the grime is. Nevertheless, when you are sad and wander around our town, you should not immediately reach for alcohol, because you can always find a spot where you will feel somewhat better. For example, where the forest begins or would begin, if it had not been cut down, there are many benches painted green on which you can sit. The people who don't like our town also find solace on these benches, as well as Father between house calls. Many of our workers (or unemployed), who are (or were) employed in our textile or iron factories, had earlier been unruly, yet now they are tamed, Herr Lohmann says to us and grins. But some are being eaten up. Do you know who is eating them up, Herr Lohmann asks from the blackboard, and looks at us. Well then, he says, when we nod. Therefore we hit back and drive away what is eating us. Is that understood? asks Herr Lohmann.

Yes, sir, we call out.

All Heidenstrasse knows that Herr Veilchenfeld is to be relocated on the weekend. Some think that he, like Herr Lilienthal, will have to be at the old depot with fifty marks in small denominations at eight o'clock in the morning; others, that, because he is a professor, he will be picked up by a limousine. Still others think that the affair can drag on until next week, because they want to wait until the festival is over and they haven't yet gathered together enough of a load to make it worthwhile. At night? By day? At dawn? No, that no one knew. Yet there is Herr Veilchenfeld, as one of our last. Frau Heuer, who lives opposite him, knows it from her husband, but where he knows it from, Frau Heuer doesn't know. Herr Heuer works at the waterworks and, on a bet, has Herr Veilchenfeld's water turned off in the middle of August, in order to see what he will do. Whether he comes and complains, or whether he puts up with it. Herr Veilchenfeld, for days without water, doesn't know what he should do. Again and again he goes over to the tap, but the water doesn't run. Finally, when Father has once again listened to his heart and his lungs and wants to go, he says to him: Oh, yes, there is no running water here.

Why not, asks Father, haven't you paid your bill?

I have, says Herr Veilchenfeld. Always.

Then Father goes into the kitchen, and the water really isn't running. Wait, he says and sits Herr Veilchenfeld on the sofa. And puts on his hat and goes to the Water Bureau and, through the long corridors and anterooms gradually penetrates to Herr Heuer and confronts him and asks directly, Herr Heuer, why have you turned off Herr Veilchenfeld's water?

Then Herr Heuer, to whom the question is embarrassing, says: Pst, not so loud! He stands up at his desk and draws Father into a corner where they can't be heard. You know, he says, you understand me right, it was a joke.

And what kind of a joke is that, Herr Heuer? asks Father.

Well, says Herr Heuer, an idea.

Yours?

Yes.

Well then, Herr Heuer, says Father, after he has regarded Herr Heuer sternly for a while, this man on whom you have played this joke is my patient. He is very sick, he must drink a great deal, and now he no longer has running water. But you probably did not consider that, right?

No, says Herr Heuer, I didn't consider it in that way.

Very well, says Father, if you did not consider it in that way, I would like to ask you to turn his water on again.

In short: That he was now to be relocated, everyone knew. Herr Weiss in the flat above the Heuers knew about it from the Town Hall, Herr Krappes from Pastor Lachmann, while Herr Greim, when he saw no light at Herr Veilchenfeld's, even thought he was already relocated, and was surprised when on Saturday the light went on again. As for Frau Ver-hören, who, as Father says, actually is named Frau *Verheuren*, on Friday—the stage was then already set up, the flags were already waving—she had seen Herr Veilchenfeld still in the garden. She could only wonder when she saw him once again on Sunday evening and she no longer nodded to him. She thought in one or two days he would no longer be with us. Even Frau Uhlmann knew of his relocation, although she had not left her flat now for a year—like Herr Magirius in his house in Russdorf. When her legs failed, she had had her bed pushed to the window and now she looked out at Heiden-strasse the entire day. Father had no objections. At least, if she can't get around any more, she sits and doesn't lie down, he says to Mother. Just don't lie down, Frau Uhlmann, just don't lie down, he exclaimed every time he examined her and was leaving. Sit instead, Frau Uhlmann, he said, sit! and threatened her with his finger. Because if you lie down, he said, and wanted to add: Soon you won't be able to stand up again, but then he let that go. At all events, Frau Uhlmann now always sat at the window and knew what was happening in our midst.

Perhaps Father is the last one who does not know that Herr Veilchenfeld is to be relocated. On Monday he was still examining him, on Tuesday he has to go to Berlin. On Wednesday, when we are alone, something very different happens. A raging storm slams into our last walnut tree and grabs the treetop and drags it out of our courtyard, over the town and the countryside and the universe, as I can distinctly see from my bed through our window, which is carefully closed and pulled tight by Mother. If I had known this, says Father, when he is back and, after dinner, we are standing next to one another at the window and, instead of the tree, as before, we are looking at both blocks of flats, then, he says, then ... But then he says no more. Has he forgotten what he wants to say, or does he realise that he too, even if he had known about the relocation, could no longer have helped Herr Veilchenfeld? For now no one can help Herr Veilchenfeld any more, not even by praying, Mother says to us. Therefore we think no more about him; we'd rather think about the festival.

The festival takes place on Sunday; everyone is warmly welcome. There's a lot that's free at the festival, for example balloons. And the pancakes that are still warm and sprinkled with powdered sugar and filled with a coffee-spoonful of marmalade and are thrown down to us from the balcony of our Town Hall. You stand in the crush and raise your hand

and call out: A pancake here please, Miss! and immediately one comes flying. Then unfortunately it's always the adults who catch it; we always miss them anyway. Other pancakes fall on the ground and are trampled. One little girl who bends down for one is knocked over and is within a hair's breadth of being trampled to death, when her father pulls her out from underfoot at the last moment. Anyway, the festival begins Sunday afternoon and lasts until Monday morning. Nothing like this has ever taken place among us before, at least not for a long time. It is a homeland festival to celebrate the founding of our town, which took place long ago; how long ago, no one knows, says Father. Therefore our founding can just as well be celebrated today as tomorrow or in five years, he says, and waves it aside. Anyway, all the adults and all the children of our town are taking part, all dressed in costumes assigned to them and in designated *families*. These are, according to their importance: the prince and princess, the prince's court, the warriors, the musicians, the farmers, the linen weavers, the woodcutters and the charcoal burners, because earlier all of these were once in our town. The older people, who don't dress up any more and can no longer get around, are given flags to wave and to put up in the house entrances. Toward the end of the festival, if it isn't raining, there will be fireworks set up so that out from the Kellerwiese, where everything ends, our houses will be wonderfully illuminated by the rockets.

Then we are walking along in the festival parade, I as a woodsman, my sister as a charcoal burner, while Father has emergency service and sits in the *Town Pharmacy* in front of the medicine cupboard and waits for the injured that such a festival brings along. While Mother sits at home by the window and looks out at the street and hopes that the festival will soon be over and we'll come home to tell her everything. My sister and I are in two different *families* and hardly see one another. I am wearing one of the woodsman's peaked hats that arrived at our school at the last moment and were distributed and put on our heads, although no one wanted to wear them because they look ridiculous and not recognisable as woodsmen's hats at all. Again and again people from other *families*, indeed even our teacher, come to us and point to our heads and ask, what kind of hats are these that you have on? Woodsmen, Herr Sperber, can't you tell? And Herr Sperber says: No, you can't tell. Soon I hate my woodsman's hat and would really like to throw it away, but that's forbidden. I hate the axe, which we woodsmen also have, even more. It is a woodsman's or woodcutter's axe; at least, it's supposed to be. So that nothing will happen, its blade is a mock blade of cardboard which, because it should be of steel, glistens with iron colouring. Because the festival was so miserably organised, the blades were distributed just at the last moment; the axe handles had to be brought by us.

What, said Mother, you don't get the handle?

No, I said, each person has to provide that.

So at the last moment, because she didn't find a handle in our cellar, Mother went with me to Rösch the carpenter and ordered one for me. Unfortunately she was not able to tell Herr Rösch how she imagined it, and so Herr Rösch didn't make me a normal straight handle, but instead, so that I would be favourably set apart from the other woodsmen, a curved and fanciful one. When we are back home again and Mother has inserted the false cardboard blade into the handle Herr Rösch made, no one knows what it is, so that I am not only asked what I am because of my hat, but also because of my axe. That spoiled the whole festival for me, though at the same time some of it was nice. For example, the windows and the balconies under which we pass by are decorated with flowers and flags and look so festive that they're completely unrecognisable. Yes, the whole town is so transformed, it's hardly recognisable. Many people who always walked around silent and grumpy, smile and even laugh at the festival and throw flowers and candies down on us and are photographed doing it. But unfortunately, they always just throw the flowers and the sweets on the princely family, and when we woodsmen and farmers and charcoal burners come, there's nothing left to be thrown. We also pass by the bay window of Herr Veilchenfeld, but here there are no flowers or flags, here there's not even a light. There are also no window panes through which one could see a shadow, and in the end as the glazier no longer wanted to see the panes that had been broken over and over again and no longer wanted to replace them either, Herr Veilchenfeld had to have the window boarded up in order to live behind the boards without a piano and without his work. Then, as we are by his garden gate, I see Herr Veilchenfeld himself. In his black coat and hat and with a cane, he is standing in his back garden, gloomy and withdrawn, with his emergency bag, and is waiting for the relocation and doesn't want anyone to see him. That's why he's stepped into the lilac bush, because no one expects him to be there, as most are just looking ahead, or above, to see whether the weather will hold. And they think Herr Veilchenfeld has already been relocated, or that he is in the back room and is having a quick nap before the limousine comes. No one suspects that he is standing in the bush by the wall, so he is not seen either. Only I see him, because I know that Herr Veilchenfeld is liable to be anywhere. I see that he is swaying somewhat and is clinging tightly to the bush and his face is completely pale, and I step out of my *family* and go to the garden gate. And then when I have looked around, and no one is looking at me, I go into the garden and behind the bush, where Herr Veilchenfeld is silently holding his bag and is already expecting me.

What is that? he asks and points to my axe.

My forest axe, I say. And I quickly point to my hat and say: And this is my woodsman's hat.

And you, asks Herr Veilchenfeld, what are you?

A woodsman.

Then you don't belong to the princely family?

No.

Well, perhaps in the next festival, in the event there is another one, says Herr Veilchenfeld. Then he emerges from the bush a little way, and while the festival parade with its brass music goes on outside, he says: Listen, Hans, do me a favour. And with his shaking white fingers he searches in his waistcoat pocket and pulls out two coins. You know that sometimes I go walking in this garden, he asks me.

Because of the fresh air, I say.

Correct, he says. And you probably also know that this year there are more vermin than usual that must go. Did you know that?

No.

Well, he says, now you know it. Beetles and snails and other things that gobble up everything and that one treads on, when one's eyes weaken.

Huh.

Like mine.

I see.

Here, take this, says Herr Veilchenfeld and gives me the coins, two five-mark pieces, I see. And take them to the pharmacy and buy me something to use against them. But don't say that it's for me; say you need it yourself. For vermin, something strong that doesn't just stun, but kills right away.

But, I say, it's my Father who's at the *Town Pharmacy*.

Then go to the other one, Herr Veilchenfeld says and is a little impatient because he thinks I don't want to do him the favour. When you have it, stick it in my letter box. You know where it is. With the rest of the money buy yourself something. Then Herr Veilchenfeld looks around quickly, and when he is certain that no one is there, he gives me a little pat on the shoulder.

Go, he says, buy it for me.

I'll buy it, I say, I'll stick it in the box. Well, then I'll go now, I say and I go and start to wave.

Well then, he says and doesn't wave.

When the sun had disappeared behind Dittrich's knitware factory and the sky and the houses and my hat and my axe could not be seen so well and I was no longer being asked what I represented in the festival parade, I heaved a sigh. Most of the shops and flats were dark when we went by them, only the Town Hall was lit up in front of us because the people who organised our festival were sitting inside. I took off the hat and jammed the axe under my woodsman's jacket and at the *Lion Pharmacy* bought something strong against vermin for Herr Veilchenfeld and threw it quickly into his box and became very cheerful afterwards. I didn't go back to my *family* any more, which had probably already forgotten me, but instead walked for a while in the last one, the giant charcoal burner family, where my sister was. She cried the whole time because she was just a charcoal burner. For she had been promised she could be a flower girl and walk at the head of the parade with a basket and scatter flowers that everyone, beginning with the Prince and Princess, would then walk over. That is, even *in front of* the elephant, which the Circus Krone had lent for the festival parade and which because of its age was completely doddery and mouldy and didn't belong in the festival parade at all. But then the Prince and Princess had changed their minds and had chosen a different flower girl and my poor little sister had simply been stuck amongst the charcoal burners. At that, the charcoal burners were the worst off; they didn't even have axes. Instead, each carried a piece of wood or a tree limb, supposedly for burning, and that wasn't even provided, but instead each charcoal burner had to bring it himself. Naturally Mother couldn't find any tree limb to burn in a hurry. Instead of that she just found a thin branch for my sister, which was much too green for burning, and then another charcoal burner took it away from her. No wonder she'd cried so much. The beard and the whiskers that Mother had painted on her, so that she would at least look a little like a charcoal burner, were completely washed away by her crying, and ran down her neck.

Don't cry, Gretel, I said again and again, but she just had to cry.

So I dropped back more and more, so that I didn't have to see her cry. Until I started walking with Gauper and Müller and Heinrich, whose fathers were all *fed up* and who represented absolutely nothing in the parade, but instead just walked along all the way at the end of the parade and made fun of everything. And probably we would have even fallen behind the street cleaners (who in order to clean up the huge amount of filth walked directly behind the festival parade with their buckets), if they hadn't prodded us with their long brooms. We were tired and yawned a lot, but the festival was just beginning.

For the festival, in the market place, long tables and benches had been set up which were to be lit up after sunset by a spotlight that stood on the Town Hall roof. So that in the mild evening air everyone could sit comfortably and smoke and eat and drink and chat pleasantly about the past and the future of our town. The tables stretched out into the surrounding streets. It is therefore possible that Herr Veilchen-feld, through his boarded-up bay window—through the cracks between the boards—could have heard and seen something of our festival; his life lasted that long. It's more likely that he didn't want to see or hear anything at all of our festival, but instead had gone to the back of his flat, that is to say, into the bedroom or the kitchen or the storage space, just to escape the festival. Perhaps he had even crawled into the book box once again. At all events Herr Veilchenfeld, if he had wanted to, *could* have still seen the festival, but surely he didn't want to. He had reached the point where he wanted nothing more at all, Father said to Mother. But we wanted to and we pushed on toward the market square, masked and made up or just as we were, and sang or made music with or against one another. Many were also drunk; some openly carried bottles in their hands. In the market, we sat or stood around the stage on which the band was to play. They had walked in, and then slipped out of, the most important place just in front of the warriors, but then they came again. To the right and left below the stage were beer barrels and in between was a sausage-and-roll stand, on which there were also potato pancakes and roasted apples to buy. From the stage Miss Schilz, who did piecework in the Schaarschmidt stocking factory and was reputed to be the greatest beauty in our town and therefore was dressed as the Princess for the occasion, was supposed to distribute paper flags, also for free, to those in the parade that would break up here. We were supposed to wave the flags in the air during the fireworks, so that from afar it could be seen how festive we were. Then there was to be dancing on a few boards in front of the *Deutscher Peter*.

But first there were still the fireworks. We stood, without pancakes but with flags, on the Kellerwiese and waited and waved our flags upwards, to where the fireworks were supposed to come, but the fireworks didn't come. What does this mean, we thought, where are the fireworks, how much longer will we have to wait? But then, just when we were thinking that they would never come, the fireworks came. First we thought it was summer lightning that was going so uncertainly across the sky, but then Müller stuck a finger in the air and said: It's the fireworks! And that's what it was, too. Because that's how fireworks begin, at least around here. As if from bolts of lightning, brightness is spread over the whole area, then come the single spheres. Not only golden ones, but also red and blue and green ones, which light up the roofs of our town, especially the church steeple roof, on which both of the roofers had hung, and then they sink very serenely over our town and over our landscape.

There are the fireworks, Heinrich said, and pointed at them.

Yes, I said, now they're starting.

You can hear them, too, said Müller, and then we heard them too.

Look, cried out Frau Sachs, who always advises Mother not to talk to Herr Veilchenfeld so much, and then Mother always says: Oh, Frau Sachs, I only say what is strictly necessary to him. Yes, but even that is too much, Frau Sachs always says then, and Mother says: Maybe you are right, Frau Sachs. Now Frau Sachs was looking up in the sky with her mouth open. Gauper and Müller and Heinrich and I were also looking up in the sky. We had separated ourselves in the birch woods from the others. And had lost my sister, probably on the way there. But maybe she was already at home, maybe she was asleep already. And *was dreaming* of the fireworks, while we were really seeing them and really hearing the bangs of the horsetail fireworks from over behind the church. Yes, those were the fireworks, that would have been it! Hopefully this one would be longer than the last one, hopefully it would never be over. The fireworks people must have been far away from us, well outside town, beyond the trees and the churches and on account of the danger, dressed in long rubber coats and high boots and with heavy helmets on their heads, and thus they sent up their spheres. They climbed higher and higher, and then they exploded and were red or green and came down again in clusters or drops, which Frau Sachs could really taste, and immersed the town in fire and light.

Ah! people cried out and: Oh! and Ooh! and our town was actually *enchanted* by the lights in the sky, as it was written in the newspaper. Naturally the enchantment did not last long, only as long as the rocket. But you didn't have to wait long before the next one came along. Anyway, the fireworks lasted much longer than the last time, but they also did not last forever, and around midnight it was over. When we had waited long enough for the next rocket and no more came, we walked away from the edge of the birch woods again and everyone was shivering. Naturally, now the fireworks were gone, what should we do? A few, instead of going home, moved toward Herr Gipser's house, with its brightly lit and wide-open windows, where the supposed founding of our town was being further celebrated until morning and you could hear the corks popping. But most went home.

We went home too. And spoke, since nothing else occurred to us, about the cost of the fireworks and the festival and how many had come to be there. Had it been a thousand, twenty thousand or, as Heinrich thought, a hundred thousand? And how much had the beer cost that they had drunk? Müller had seen eighty crates, Gauper a hundred and fifty, Heinrich even three hundred. Added to that the barrels that were continuously rolled back and forth between the *Deutscher Peter* and the stage and that no one had counted, not even Müller. Then the rockets that we'd all seen but had not counted, and the number of which we now estimated. Gauper thought there had been a hundred, Müller eighty and fifty horsetail fireworks, Heinrich forty rockets and eighty horsetail fireworks. I thought three hundred, both together. Then the stage, the benches, the paper lanterns, the decoration of the streets. Müller thought that everything altogether had cost ten thousand, Gauper, twenty thousand, and Heinrich, that it had cost a million. I just said that it had probably been expensive, because Mother had forbidden me to talk about money with other people.

We went home and walked across the market, which opened wide toward the stars. But, apart from the moon and the stars in the sky, there was nothing more going on there now. Under the sky lay the town, silent and motionless, because now the spotlight on the Town Hall roof and most of the streetlights were switched off. For that reason our steps rang out louder than before, because the town was now so quiet, even if it was also not yet asleep. For even a few shops were still open. People who were speaking once more about the festival and what they had seen, who wanted once more to *chew the fat*, stood around on the street corners. The stage and the tables and the benches were deserted, Helenenstrasse was empty, and bottles and flags and apple cores lay around on the pavements. Only off in the distance someone was still singing, but you couldn't see him. Or a little, till now overlooked rocket was quickly sent into the sky, or at the edge of town we heard a guitar, playing a serenade there. But then someone immediately shouted for quiet, and the guitar had to move on. Then we had the market behind us and came into Heidenstrasse, and there Herr Rösch came upon us and stood in front of us and asked me if I was who he thought, and I said yes. Then Herr Rösch asked me how I knew who he was thinking that I was, and I said I don't know, I just assumed. Then Herr Rösch thought for a while and said: Aha, and asked me if I was satisfied with my axe and where was it now. Then I reached into my woodsman's jacket and pulled out the axe and said: Satisfied, Herr Rösch, satisfied, the axe was outstanding.

I hope so, because it was a lot of trouble for me, Herr Rösch said. Then he pushed Gauper and Müller and Heinrich a little way down the street and came a little closer still and pointed up to the flat of Herr Veilchenfeld and asked me if I still saw "the gentleman upstairs there" as often.

But I don't see him often at all, Herr Rösch, I almost never see him, I said.

And I thought you knew each other and saw each other all the time.

No.

And your father isn't friends with him?

But not at all, I said, he just listens to his heart.

Very well, said Herr Rösch, it's just about his furniture that I would like to have when he is relocated. Do you think the furniture is still upstairs?

That I don't know.

And if he's already been relocated, you don't know that either?

No, I said, I don't know that either. But if you ask me, then I believe he is still upstairs.

But it's completely dark, said Herr Rösch, how can he still be upstairs there?

Oh, the darkness doesn't bother him. He's used to it.

And how do you know that, if you don't know him?

I think so.

And that he's still upstairs?

Sometimes I see him hurry by.

Although everything is boarded up?

Oh, I see him anyway.

Very well, maybe you see him through the cracks, said Herr Rösch and went on in the direction of the *Lampenputzer*, which was not at all where his carpentry workshop

was. His workshop was in the other direction, but he didn't
go that way. Gauper and Müller and Heinrich also went on,
I followed them then. And said: "So long, all of you!" and
poked them in the ribs and went home and got undressed
and lay down in my bed, but without falling asleep; I just
lay there.

The house where Herr Veilchenfeld lives belongs to a Frau
Belling, whom no one has ever seen, some even say she may
be dead. But that's not right, Frau Belling is living, and indeed
in Grüna in the institution, which she will never leave again
either, Father says to Mother and to us. He knows this from
the institution's doctor, who once talked to him about her
in front of the Klemm pastry shop. For example, she can no
longer hold her water, but that would not be so bad, if she
did not also *trickle away in the head* and no longer know
who she is or who others are and in what year we are all
living. (When she is asked, she simply says it is *too late*.) And
so like her head, her house is also deteriorating and no longer
holds together, because she no longer has anything fixed,
even though it is necessary. For example, the iron fence,
which is so rusted that it will simply collapse, should be
painted. The stairs are worn and smooth and deep like basins,
and the shingles on the roof... No, Father says nothing about
the shingles! It is as if Frau Belling in "Sonnenblick" lets her
house, like herself, deliberately go to rack and ruin. At the
same time, she had promised Herr Veilchenfeld, when he
moved in, *a complete restoration*—otherwise she would have
found no tenant—but then thought no more about it. Later
he was put off again and again; now they don't answer him
at all any more. Instead, Frau Belling's future heirs, who are

twins and who live in a two-winged villa in Russdorf and wear identical suits and ties and shoes and have identical haircuts and gladly let themselves be confused, even by their wives, are waiting now for two things: for Herr Veilchenfeld's relocation and for Frau Belling's death at the institution. And then they will immediately pull down the house and have something larger built in its place, perhaps a modern cinema or a petrol station, because there is space, says Father. Also no one bothered with the rear garden and the beanpoles, which the tenant before Herr Veilchenfeld must have forgotten and which Herr Veilchenfeld, until his end, continually thrust back into the ground. Because Frau Belling is still living, everything must run to seed.

Father is the first to find out, for professional reasons. Frau Abfalter, once again at his place to clean, walks unsuspecting into Herr Veilchenfeld's flat at dawn and, after she has hung up her coat and taken off her street shoes, has a horrifying experience. After she has regarded the corpse for a while with tilted head and put her coat and street shoes back on, she comes directly to us. She knows a death, in order to count, must be verified, and that by Father, in writing, and she finds our house at once. If she stumbled upon the body around six, she is at our house at a quarter to seven. But our bell hasn't worked for days and no one hears her knocking—we are trying to forget the homeland festival, to sleep the homeland festival to its death—so she steps beneath our parents' bedroom window and begins to call. Doctor, she calls, first quietly, then louder, then altogether recklessly. Finally, she throws stones at the window.

When Father hears the stones, he thinks: Not again! and

sits up in bed. But then he hears they are little stones, and calms down. When the stones don't stop, he swings himself out of bed and, with his hair unkempt and with his crutch, so without his left leg, hops out of his dream—he doesn't tell us out of which one—to the window and sticks his head out. Then Frau Abfalter drops the stones that she still has in her hand, she is so startled by his appearance. She also doesn't say good morning. When she has composed herself again and cleared her throat, she calls, Father should come quickly to 26 Heidenstrasse, something needs certifying there.

Hello, who is speaking down there then, calls Father, who without his glasses at dawn can certainly perceive something, but can't recognise Frau Abfalter, whom he knows only in passing.

Oh, it's Frau Abfalter speaking, she says then from below, from Herr Veilchenfeld.

Then Father recognises her.

But Frau Abfalter, don't you know what time it is, says Father, who doesn't know himself and is still stuck in his dream. And he holds his sleeping jacket closed around himself against the morning wind, which always blows around our house at this time. You come to me at such a time, just for me to certify something? What should I certify, then?

Then Frau Abfalter says, it is on account of Herr Veilchenfeld, because now Herr Veilchenfeld is dead.

Oh, says Father and staggers a little and holds the window frame tightly for a moment, because of his one leg. Then he says: So you are here . . .

Yes, she says, I stepped in, and then I stumbled upon him.

Very well, I will come then, says Father very quietly, because he has meanwhile remembered that he does not want to be upset about the life and death of his patients, even when it makes him sorry, and he clears his throat just a little. This throat clearing also wakes our Mother.

So who is it, she asks Father.

Frau Abfalter, says Father, from Herr Veilchenfeld.

And what does she want?

Oh, he says, Herr Veilchenfeld is dead, just go back to sleep.

Whereas Father, as a doctor, naturally has duties and cannot sleep any longer. Instead he pulls his leg out from under the bed and attaches it and slips into his shirt from yesterday and his trousers and jacket and kisses Mother on the cheek in parting as usual. And, after he has put on his hunter's hat in the hall and has taken his stick, he drives through our still inanimate town to Heidenstrasse in his automobile beside Frau Abfalter, who already has her rubber apron on under her coat. While I, despite my shock, must have gone to sleep again, until as a sign of the new day it becomes light, first over our jam factory and then in our room. And the people across in the blocks of flats wake up and get out of their beds and make noise and push open the windows, so that you can also hear their noise. This noise wakes me up and I find out for a second time—I forgot it while sleeping—that Herr Veilchenfeld is dead.

Father must have quickly shaken off his dream and hurriedly entered the flat in Heidenstrasse. He wanted to have this behind him.

I might have nearly fallen and possibly even broken something, when I wanted to cross the threshold, he said to Mother, when he told her everything later in the kitchen.

Herr Veilchenfeld's flat was open, like the flats of all people who depart from us overnight, but no one had been there who had touched or pocketed anything or thrown anything against the wall; the furniture is also still there. Because Father is afraid to have Frau Abfalter close by his side during the post-mortem, restricting him or shoving or even just observing, he puts his hand on her shoulder and pushes her aside.

Not so close, Frau Abfalter, that is not necessary, I know my way, he says. Here, sit for a while in the kitchen and make yourself coffee.

Would you like some too? Frau Abfalter asks Father.

Yes, make me some too, says Father to Frau Abfalter, I haven't had any yet.

And how would you like it?

Oh, it doesn't matter, but without sugar, says Father to Frau Abfalter and pushes her into the kitchen. Then he closes the door behind her and gets down to work.

He opens his doctor's bag and, instead of the stethoscope that he always placed on Herr Veilchenfeld's chest, he pulls out the forms that he naturally has with him too, in the event a case should become hopeless. And with the forms in his hand, he goes through the flat. As he forgot to ask Frau Abfalter in which room she stumbled upon Herr Veilchenfeld, he will now have to go from room to room and look for him. On this Monday, because Herr Veilchenfeld is dead, these rooms, all of which Father of course knows well, have something that weighs on him, on his head and his breast and his shoulders. In the first room he goes into, it already presses down on him. Although he looks around closely, he doesn't recognise the room for a long time. Instead he must really fight his way through the unexpected disquiet that suddenly lies on the walls and chairs and lamps of the room, or hangs from them, and when he goes through or passes by, it gets caught on his clothes and hands and thoughts. But Father clenches his teeth and fights through the disquiet hanging down around him. In that way, although he doesn't find Herr Veilchenfeld for a long time, he makes some interesting discoveries. It seems, for example, as though Herr Veilchenfeld, who never did explain his philosophy to Father and in the end perhaps no longer had one at all, by dragging himself through all these rooms and tearing up all these rooms in his death throes, had died in them all. Father believes he stumbles over traces of this death that was equally spread everywhere in the entire flat; everywhere he encounters articles touched by the death of Herr Veilchenfeld. Yes, of course, it was poison, Father thinks, and that it was best for him, and he could smell the poison, as well as Herr Veilchenfeld, in all the rooms. And then, when Herr Veilchenfeld took the poison, he was agitated over what now would come directly—his death—repeatedly going in and out of his various rooms and leaving his distress and his oppression behind in the rooms—spread amongst the individual rooms. As if he could not decide in which room he wanted to conclude his existence, Father said to Mother in the evening, when dinner was finally on the table, when he put back the bread he had already taken and cut and said: There is more. In addition, dust is everywhere, he said, and meant Herr Veilchenfeld's flat, which he, the form in his hand, wanders through after him. Everywhere the wardrobes were ripped open and the drawers pulled out and the laundry ransacked, and everything was lying about, as if someone else had already been there before Father. And after so many years without movement, Herr Veilchenfeld must have felt once again a great urge to move and must have hurried through his flat many times with his coat-tails flying. But this doesn't surprise me, says Father to Mother, he always went somewhat faster than he could. Later, as with all who are poisoned, the need to drink, the *thirst for the Dardanelles*, must have come, there are glasses everywhere. In the bedroom, next to the doll's bed, there was even a flower vase lying on its side, out of which Herr Veilchenfeld perhaps had drunk and which he then would have laid down: there is a puddle on the floor. While in the kitchen the water is running and an old dog blanket lies on the tiles, in which he must have wrapped himself, like someone who is going out into the cold. For at the end he would have been frozen and sweating and the walls and the windows and the clock and all the other things in the room just blurry, as if perceived through a frosted pane, Father recounts. Yes, so they say, he says to me, as if through a frosted pane. Then he vomited and spat blood, there are also traces of that present, which Father follows, somewhat bent over, because it is still dark, because otherwise he would lose the traces. Until Herr Veilchenfeld decided on his cabinet and resolved to die on his sofa among the remainder of his books, Father says to Mother in the evening, in our kitchen where it was dark for such a long time, and he tells her how he follows him.

So instead of the black limousine to relocate him, there are the pall bearers, with whip drawn, here on the 18th of September, a Monday, around ten. The sky carries rain over us in unsettled, elongated clouds. In any case, because of the homeland festival, I don't have to go to school yet. Instead we are standing in front of Höhler's garden fence and not making ourselves dirty and we look first at the clouds and then up the street. Everywhere people are leaning out their windows, some are still flying flags.

And that? asks my sister.

The hearse.

Why?

Oh, for him, I say. Come, I'll show it to you. And I take her hand, and we go across the street, which has a hump here so that the rain runs off. Since it's raining now, we can hear it, but we don't feel it yet. We go under the apple trees, which keep the rain off us.

Have you ever seen a cabinet, I ask my sister.

No, she says, is there one here?

Yes, I say, upstairs. And point to Herr Veilchenfeld's house. Do you want to?

I don't mind.

And then, when we have walked around the horse and around the carriage a few times and also touched the carriage—not the horse—and wiped our fingers off again, and hung about under the apple trees some and from the courtyard gate studied everything some more—no one is calling us, no one is shouting at us—we go quickly into the courtyard and over the cobblestones of the courtyard to the wide-open front door. Grass is growing between the cobblestones. From the building, the thudding of the folding machine in Lamprecht's cardboard box company.

It will be closed up at the end of the year, and then they will demolish the building, Mother says to Father and to me. Then in that place a hole will be dug and something else erected, but what, she doesn't know. Do the two workers from Lamprecht's know that there was a philosopher living above them, who in the end no longer left the house and now is dead? I walk into the house, my sister remains standing in front of the house.

Is it inside there? she asks.

Yes, I say.

And then, after my sister has walked over to me in the stairwell and looked around and hesitated for a long time, I take her hand and say: It's time.

What?

To look at it. Come on, just up the stairs. Come on, walk behind me.

The hall is musty, the stairwell almost black. Then five, six steps straight ahead.

You're going too slowly, I say and pull her after me. If you go this slowly, we'll never see it. And I climb a couple of steps again and stretch out my neck and stay close to the wall, so that no one sees me, in case someone is looking from above. And I climb farther, she behind me, above us the hearse drivers. The steps first creak under them, then they creak under us.

Is that it, asks my sister.

No, I say, that's not it.

The hearse drivers put down the empty coffin against the stairwell wall in front of Herr Veilchenfeld's flat. They take off their strange caps equipped with tassels, already familiar to me from Grandfather's funeral—but not to my sister—and want to knock on the glass in the door. But then, before they can, Frau Abfalter appears, shuffling. She must have heard something in the stairwell and comes out of the kitchen in her rubber apron. And, because she doesn't want to touch anything at Herr Veilchenfeld's, she pushes the flat door open with the broom handle. She probably knows the hearse drivers from the cemetery, anyway she winks at them.

Rain, the hearse drivers say in greeting, their caps in their hands.

Since early morning, answers Frau Abfalter.

Well then, say the hearse drivers.

In the cabinet, she says.

And because the coffin doesn't fit through the door of the flat, she pulls the door bolts up and folds back the whole front panel. Then the flat stands wide open.

Come, I say to my sister.

It smells so here, she says.

Oh, smells, I say, and reach for her hand, but she pulls her hand back, and only after I've grabbed at it two or three more times does she let me take it, and we climb up higher. And we look through the balusters at how the hearse drivers, who have now put their caps back on, first break into the corridor with their coffin and then into Herr Veilchenfeld's cabinet, which because of the boards in front of the windows is his darkest room. It's behind the door, I say.

What, she asks.

The cabinet, I say.

Where I have been twice, my sister never. And where Herr Veilchenfeld, since he turned up here three years before, spent most of his time and where you saw him through his window when you looked up. Here at one of his tables he sat over his work. Until, because there was nothing more to heat with, his fingers froze, although he finally wore gloves even when he was writing, says Father, who prescribed an ointment for his chilblains. There was now no longer any talk of piano playing, and he also could no longer continue with the work in which he had been so very *caught up* in warmer times, because of his *thoughts of nothingness* (Father), but instead he pushed it away from himself ever further, first to the middle, and then past the middle, of his table in the bay. And he sat in the cold and in the dark and let the time pass by and he saw how his philosophy dissolved amidst his boredom and his fear of death, Father says. He hardly even drummed on the empty table top with his frozen fingers, so that he could at least hear himself in the surrounding silence, he said. And now he must be gotten out of here, and quickly, indeed, because he had let himself deteriorate, and his cabinet too.

I am in a house of death, we climb up the steps. One landing already lies behind us, the stairwell window too. In the garden, under the apple tree, a person is walking around, his shadow flickers on the wall and becomes longer and then shorter again and then disappears. But we will now see Herr Veilchenfeld's cabinet, maybe even Herr Veilchenfeld himself. He lived behind his boarded-up windows like an old rabbit and without work, says Father, when he cannot eat anything at dinner one day. What a disgrace this house represents for our town, a normal person can hardly imagine, Herr Lohmann says to the barber, who must shave his neck closely. No, don't use this razor, use the other, he says. What should one say if a stranger comes and goes past it by chance and asks what kind of a house that is and who lives in it and why it looks the way it does, he asks. Herr Lohmann also has his chin and his throat shaved, so that on the next morning he will walk through our classroom like a convict—Müller says: like a bull. And now Frau Abfalter, who has probably not been in Herr Veilchenfeld's cabinet for weeks, and thus should have been ashamed of its condition, tries to quickly straighten up a little for the two hearse drivers. She hurriedly shoves something under the sofa, so no one will fall over it, for Herr Veilchenfeld let it lie there out of pure lethargy. And how often toward the end did he forget to wash himself! Ever since he had once neglected to get undressed before going to sleep, he had the same shirt and the same trousers on day and night. So he was really unkempt then. He no longer noticed the dirt on his books that had been exposed to the weather. Merciful dirt, you that lay yourself on books, merciful darkness! At the same time, he still had eyes in completely good order for his age, even if by the end the right lid no longer went up, but rather had to be raised by his finger at the relevant moment because of muscle paralysis. Like this, says Father and shows us. He was also more and more silent, and now he is completely silent and must be disposed of.

The manner of the disposal is whispered about behind the cabinet door. Just away, away, away from here! In the narrow cabinet how hurriedly then he is laid in the coffin, which is still narrower! But we don't see this, after all the door is in between, and we're standing on the next flight of steps, by the attic door. Then the lid is closed with a snap; that we can hear well.

Was that the cabinet, my sister asks.

No, I say, that was he himself. They've put the lid over him.

And why isn't he nailed in?

So he can come out, if he wants to.

Will he want to?

No.

Then, as we stand on the attic stairs on this Monday in September and I want to show my sister Herr Veilchenfeld's cabinet, the hearse drivers take him out; they leave the door open behind them. Then we have to climb still higher so that they don't see us. Because they now know the way, things go more easily with the coffin. Under Frau Abfalter's direction they carry the coffin back out of the cabinet, which is now empty. And how empty it is! Silent, says Father, silent. And now, he says, let us think for one moment about the renowned overwhelming emptiness in all death chambers, about the sudden vacuum, he says to Mother and to us. But then, as we are completely silent and have our eyes shut for a long time, and have thought about the emptiness, as Father directed us, we see the cabinet is not empty at all. Out of the bay recess two dark men, whom we could not see at all from our attic step until now, are suddenly marching in step. They have broad hats on and wear leather coats that are buckled in front. They probably crawled along the bay shelves, but now they have stood up and brushed off their coats. Then they walk along the other shelves to the other books, which we can see well through the two open doors. And they reach with their hands—they have leather gloves on—deep into the books that are still there. They pull out many and pile them on the middle table, which Herr Rösch now will soon lacquer; others they throw on the floor. And they point out Herr Veilchenfeld's books to one another and nod or shake their heads. Until, when they are already standing in books to their ankles, they see us looking. Then they shout: Hey! And: What are you looking at? Or: Hey, who are you?

Oh, our father is the doctor, I say. He's certified everything here.

What?

That he's dead now.

Do you live here?

No, by the stone quarry.

And what are you doing here?

Nothing, we're just standing around.

Then they shout: Go away! And: Get lost! And threaten us with their leather fists.

But we're just going, I say.

But the men don't believe us, they come after us. We see how the books, through which they're wading, are crushed behind them. Then they close the cabinet door. Since we can't see the cabinet any more, we leave. There, a flight of stairs below us, are the hearse drivers with the coffin; they make a racket down the wooden steps and are wheezing and asking each other if they have him too.

I have him, one calls out. And you?

I have him too, the other calls out.

Meanwhile Frau Abfalter is behind them and calls out over and over: You, Fritz, a little higher! And: You, Wilhelm, now you also! And at the same time, because she helps at the cemetery, she sometimes looks like an already partly discarded corpse herself, says Father to Mother and to us.

Was that everything? asks my sister.

Yes, I say, that was it.

And I climb back down the stairs and she comes behind me. The shadow of the man on the wall is now no longer there. But when we want to get by Frau Abfalter and the coffin, she raises a rubber hand and says: Stop!

Good morning, Frau Abfalter, we say.

Hello, says Frau Abfalter. So what are you looking for here?

Nothing, we're not looking for anything.

Then get out, and fast, she says. But don't go past the coffin, because that doesn't bring good luck. Do you understand?

Yes, I say, but I have already, and my sister too. We've already squeezed by the coffin. Then because we have, Frau Abfalter quickly sends a couple of curses after us and with her long arms drives us out of the house and into the freedom of the rear courtyard as far as the garden wall, which has gaps at its base. Now we can no longer hope for good luck.

We're sorry, I call out.

The coffin wants to return to the daylight, but will it be able to? And if Father was mistaken and Herr Veilchenfeld is still alive? I hear how he moans and sighs and turns in his coffin.

Do you hear, I say to my sister. He's looking at us.

Through the wood? she asks.

Yes.

But the coffin does get through the narrow front door after all. Then the coffin glides, directed by Frau Abfalter, into the rear courtyard. We had such courtyards at that time. And because it contains our philosopher, it seems to have become, not only heavier (that would be natural), but also longer (that would be supernatural). It hardly gets around the corner of the house, although now Frau Abfalter is also applying a couple of rubber fingers. And it is dragged across the rear courtyard under the eyes of the neighbours, who meanwhile have all fetched their pillows and set themselves up on their window ledges and heedlessly thrust their heads into Heidenstrasse. And then, beyond the rusted courtyard gate, into Heidenstrasse. In fact, from the garden wall we could follow everything very well. The coffin is shoved into the hearse, probably with Herr Veilchenfeld's head—his *Overworld*—first. Then there is a break. The courtyard gate, the sky, the hearse drivers, everything takes a break, every-thing breathes a sigh.

Come, Gretel, I say, but she doesn't want to come. Come, I say and pull her.

Hand in hand, in step, without overtaking the coffin, out of the rear courtyard, my sister rigid with terror, Frau Ab-falter is taking off the rubber gloves, the hearse drivers are closing the courtyard gate, the neighbours are pointing out the coffin, which under a fast moving sky is in the hearse that is spacious above but also comfortable on all other sides, and like our shops in Helenenstrasse has glass showcase windows, so that you can see the flowers and the wreaths as well as the coffin, but there are no flowers and wreaths, so that the windows are covered with curtains and we can no longer see the now dead Herr Veilchenfeld. When, pulled by the little black horse, he rolls away from us, out of the town.

A Note on the Text

Many of the person and place names in Our Philosopher *consist of German nouns and adjectives, and thus have an additional meaning for anyone reading the novel in German.*
—E. M.-T.

Abfalter: Abfall = rubbish. Also ab + Falter: ex-butterfly
Berger: salvager
Birken: birch
Blei: lead
Deutscher Peter: German Peter
Eisen-Lotse: iron pilot
Geier: vulture
Gipser: plasterer
Grimmschen: adjective form of Grimm, name of the German collectors of fairy tales
Hafermeier: oats steward
Heiden: heaths, but also heathens, Gentiles
Hellmann: bright or light man
Heuer: this year; pay
Hirsch: deer. Frequently, although not always, a Jewish family name.
Höhle: cave, cavity
Keller: cellar (or a proper name)
Klemm: Klemme = a fix, a difficult situation

Krappes: Krapp = madder plant (used for making red dye)

Lach: laughter

Lampenputzer: lamp cleaner

Laube: arbour or arcade

Lauge: lye

Lilienthal: valley of lilies. Often a Jewish family name.

Linde: linden tree

Lohen: to blaze

Magirius: Magirius is Latinised from Ancient Greek μάγειρος (mágeiros), cook

Malz: malt

Maurer: mason, bricklayer

Mausifalli: Mausefalle = mousetrap

Neumann: new man

Obermüller: head miller

Raabe: raven

Reichmann: rich man

Rösch: crisp, crust

Rüdesheim: male dog + home (also a place name)

Russdorf: soot village

Sachs: Sache = item, matter, cause

Schellenbaum: bell tree (a musical instrument); also Schellen + Baum: clamps + tree

Schindler: roofer (obsolete)

Sonnenblick: sun view

Sperber: sparrow hawk

Stöcke: sticks

Turnvater Jahn (Friedrich Ludwig Jahn): founder of the Turnsport (gymnastics) movement in the early nineteenth century, considered the father of gymnastics in Germany.

Übeleis: evil or severe + ice

Veilchenfeld: field of violets

Verhören: to interrogate, question
Weiss: white
Wikinger: Viking

OTHER NEW YORK REVIEW CLASSICS

For a complete list of titles, visit www.nyrb.com.

CLAUDE ANET Ariane, A Russian Girl

HANNAH ARENDT Rahel Varnhagen: The Life of a Jewish Woman

DIANA ATHILL Don't Look at Me Like That

POLINA BARSKOVA Living Pictures

HENRI BOSCO The Child and the River

DINO BUZZATI The Stronghold

CAMILO JOSÉ CELA The Hive

EILEEN CHANG Written on Water

FRANÇOIS-RENÉ DE CHATEAUBRIAND Memoirs from Beyond the Grave, 1800–1815

LUCILLE CLIFTON Generations: A Memoir

COLETTE Chéri *and* The End of Chéri

JÓZEF CZAPSKI Memories of Starobielsk: Essays Between Art and History

ANTONIO DI BENEDETTO The Silentiary

HEIMITO VON DODERER The Strudlhof Steps

FERIT EDGÜ The Wounded Age *and* Eastern Tales

MICHAEL EDWARDS The Bible and Poetry

ROSS FELD Guston in Time: Remembering Philip Guston

BEPPE FENOGLIO A Private Affair

WILLIAM GADDIS The Letters of William Gaddis

NATALIA GINZBURG Family *and* Borghesia

JEAN GIONO The Open Road

VASILY GROSSMAN The People Immortal

MARTIN A. HANSEN The Liar

ELIZABETH HARDWICK The Uncollected Essays of Elizabeth Hardwick

UWE JOHNSON Anniversaries

ERNST JÜNGER On the Marble Cliffs

MOLLY KEANE Good Behaviour

PAUL LAFARGUE The Right to Be Lazy

JEAN-PATRICK MANCHETTE The N'Gustro Affair

THOMAS MANN Reflections of a Nonpolitical Man

MAXIM OSIPOV Kilometer 101

KONSTANTIN PAUSTOVSKY The Story of a Life

MARCEL PROUST Swann's Way

ALEXANDER PUSHKIN Peter the Great's African: Experiments in Prose

RUMI Gold; translated by Haleh Liza Gafori

FELIX SALTEN Bambi; or, Life in the Forest

ANNA SEGHERS The Dead Girls' Class Trip

VICTOR SERGE Last Times

ANTON SHAMMAS Arabesques

CLAUDE SIMON The Flanders Road

WILLIAM GARDNER SMITH The Stone Face

VLADIMIR SOROKIN Telluria

JEAN STAFFORD Boston Adventure

GEORGE R. STEWART Storm

ADALBERT STIFTER Motley Stones

ITALO SVEVO A Very Old Man

MAGDA SZABÓ The Fawn

SUSAN TAUBES Lament for Julia

TEFFI Other Worlds: Peasants, Pilgrims, Spirits, Saints

YŪKO TSUSHIMA Woman Running in the Mountains

EDITH WHARTON Ghosts: Selected and with a Preface by the Author